The
Arid Road
Home

J. P. Greene

THE ARID ROAD HOME
by J. P. Greene

Copyright © 2021 Joshua Paul Greene

Published by Wilderwest Press, 2022

This book was set in 12 pt Goudy Old Style

10 9 8 7 6 5 4 3 2

Printed in the United States of America on acid-free paper. For
information write J. P. Greene at Josh@wilderwestdigital.com

ISBN 978-1-0879-6522-2

Paperback – First Edition

PUBLISHER'S NOTE:
This is a work of fiction. Names, characters, places, and
incidents either are the product of the author's imagination or are
used fictitiously, and any resemblance to actual persons, living or
dead, events, or locales is entirely coincidental.

Cover image courtesy of Photo Boards (@createandbloom) used
under license from Unsplash.

Wilderness is not a luxury
but a necessity of the human
spirit, and as vital to our lives as
water and good bread.

-Edward Abbey, *Desert Solitaire*

This book is dedicated to
Esmé, Indra and Xander. May you always
find your way towards your own personal
truth.

Prologue

He awoke to the birdsongs and the first light of dawn. Streaming through his window, past the muslin curtains, were the quiet sounds of a waking town. Chickens clucked, bells on shop doors rang as their proprietors began the morning work, and far off he thought he could hear a dog barking.

As the breeze lifted the curtains from the window ever so slightly, he caught glimpses of the town square, where he sometimes played chess at the stone-topped tables beneath the cedar trees.

Beyond the empty, waiting benches and chairs, he could just see the chapel. He smiled upon seeing it and drew a filling breath.

Next to him, stirring slightly, lay the woman of his dreams, her almond-honey hair adrift on the pillow beneath her head like ringlet waves on a sunset shore. Across her lips lay the hint of the kiss they shared before departing into sleep, and he was tempted to place another.

But, instead, he tenderly swung his feet off the edge of the bed and sat, hunched in his grogginess, as the morning steeped into him.

Closing his eyes, sitting between the comforts of sleep and the day ahead, Joseph allowed his mind to meander over each of the near-innumerable ways in which his life had turned out better than he ever could have imagined.

He chuckled, thinking of the life he'd lived, the struggles he'd faced, and the happy accidents that had delivered him to this beautiful morning. This is a good place to be, he thought to himself, smiling.

Then he rose and walked across the cracked tile floor to the basin to splash some water on his face.

Part I

Batting the dirt off of his clothes, he stood up. The bar owner was yelling something nearly indistinguishable through his thick, black moustache, but Joseph wasn't listening. He'd heard this speech a thousand times in front of a thousand bars. At twenty-three he'd already spent enough time avoiding the painful memories that it didn't even cross his mind to consider who he'd become.

It was the darkest of nights. Stars shone brightly against a moonless sky, but he couldn't see them for the blindness induced by alcohol and the sting in his eyes from the cigar smoke of the tavern. The door of the bar slammed shut. He found himself alone. The abandoned depth of the small, dusty town in the heart of the American west imposed its foreboding upon him as he stumbled off to nowhere in particular.

As he walked, a chill wind signaled the coming winter. It was only late August but the mountains to the east carried forewarning of a long, cold season to come. Someone in the bar had told him that. He could remember that part. He'd laughed in the man's face telling him it was childish to predict the future based on the weather, but now he set himself to hoping the man wasn't right. Cold winters are hard on wanderers.

On the draft he detected a voice – a voice and a scent that smelled like the neck of a woman. Turning round as he shuffled through the dust, he saw no follower. Whispering winds surrounded him, but like the bar owner's cursing, Joseph couldn't understand a word of what was said. He shrugged it off. A boy listening to the wind. What shit, he thought to himself.

It seemed that with each dreary, pointless day that passed, his life became less and less worth living. The tedium, the endless stumbling through days and weeks and months and years. It was better than thinking about all that had happened though. Yes, he thought, it was better than to think of all that.

How long had it been, he wondered, since he had not longed for death?

By this time he was reaching the edge of town. Feeling suddenly content to wander off into the surrounding desert and meet a quiet, meaningless end amongst a million things already dead, he passed a church made of stone and adobe, humble in size but beautiful. He paused to gaze upon it, the light from a few vigil candles painting dancing shadows against the stained glass. Something tugged on his heart. But he ignored it and kept walking.

As he walked, he closed his eyes, stumbling forward with no direction, no destination. He had left the town behind, another town behind him now, a great emptiness before and inside him. He had traveled perhaps twenty feet into the desert wilderness when, rounding a large outcropping of rocks, he felt the hair on the back of his neck stand on end and a chill run across his forehead.

In what seemed an impossibly short instant he found himself knocked sideways by the blunt force of something cold and unforgiving against his head. His eyes flew open as he fell, and he had just enough time to see a hardened face. Set deep in the stranger's complexion were a ruthless pair of eyes which seemed to threaten death upon anyone who dared to look at them. Another blow hit him hard in the ribs. He felt all the breath leave his chest in the searing pain of fracturing bones as he hit the ground.

Face down with dirt between his teeth, he saw the shadow of a man come over him and deliver a final blow to the left side of his jaw. He saw the blood fly before he tasted it, but before long he could comprehend nothing but a hot river of metal dripping from his lips. Vision danced behind his eyes for a brief moment, and then he lost consciousness.

He'd not had even the opportunity to understand what was happening before he was delivered into the respite of adrenaline-fueled shock, sleep and drunkenness. All was dark and spinning. The desert around him sang peaceful, merciless songs. Then nothingness.

For days he lay there, lilting in and out of sleep. Once he awoke to find buzzards circling overhead, and when he roused later, he found one of them sitting at his feet, watching him. In weakness and shortness of breath he'd been unable to scare it off before he once again succumbed to the coma.

Another time, he had inhaled the strong scent of urine and had been able to turn his head just enough to notice numerous sets of large animal tracks surrounding him. Maybe he'd soiled himself. Or maybe an animal had done it to him. It didn't matter. Maybe he wasn't even living anymore.

After no fewer than five days, he discovered himself alert and staring through the waxing sickle of a pearlescent moon, unable to move, but by some miraculous grace no longer aching from the pain of broken bones. On the wind he smelled the smoke of desert juniper and cedar. He couldn't tell whether he was hallucinating or if a fire crackled nearby, and he could not move his head to look. From the corner of his eye, he caught a glimpse of a dark and weathered-looking man stooping, balanced on the balls of naked feet and watching him with what appeared to be the wing of a large raptor held in one hand gently blowing an intoxicating breeze over him. But before he could examine this bizarre vision, he was lulled into submission by an incredible urge to release, and to rest.

Behind his lidded eyes, he saw his childhood play out before him. The violence and the drinking and the dance of it all like some hellish ball that would never end. And how he couldn't do anything to stop it. To save her. To make it stop. To make him stop. How he had run from the house under the blanket of night, desperate to escape from the hell into which he'd been unwillingly born.

Then a flash and a montage of blurred images and he found himself standing outside the home of a woman he'd loved, inches from the door but unable to knock.

Her name was Ellie. She'd been married already, submissive to a husband whose temper matched his drinking habit, but she'd refused to leave him. And he couldn't help her either. The last night he'd seen her before setting off on this self-destructive journey to numb the pain of a lost young love, she had told him that love follows duty, and that's the way it must remain. He had wanted to argue, to explain that love and duty could not be more separate, but he'd learned better than to argue with a woman.

And so he'd started drinking, too, because that's just what people did when they couldn't face the world they knew. His father had taught him that and he'd learned it from his father. His father also taught him that women wouldn't ever listen unless you made them. But he wouldn't follow that legacy. He'd never hit them. He couldn't.

Laying in the sand, the smoke of some mysterious fire wafting above and around him, he saw these visions and many others, and in brief moments of cognition he felt sure he was experiencing his life in review, and that he must be moments from death.

The thought soothed him, allowing him to relax into receptivity to all he experienced. He fell deeper into his trance, and the images began to speed by. As faster and faster they flashed, the stream of thoughts seemed to knit themselves together into a sort of all-encompassing memory – or perhaps more of an intuition of the past; that which can be experienced, internalized, but never fully understood.

The furious shower of images overwhelmed him, and eventually he surrendered, his awareness melting with the deluge of recollection.

In what could have been weeks, or perhaps only hours, he woke finally into the dawn of a new day. Stiff from his immobility and desperately dehydrated, gaunt and weak from the compulsory fasting of unconsciousness, he roused just as a still, warm sunlight emerged over the endless expanse of desert in which he had surely died and returned to life.

He sat up slowly, feeling his cracked lips, his jaw, his ribs, and looked around. He discovered himself still positioned on a bed of sand surrounded by the same rocks which had harbored his assailant. His pockets had been turned inside out, which he thought made sense, and his shirt had been ripped up the side where his ribs had been kicked in. The latter discovery confused him.

In a daze, he stared in silence contemplating the desert and longing for it to share with him the secrets of this experience, since he could not manage to recall any of it himself.

When met with nothing but silence and the reflection of his dismay, he surrendered himself to the arduous task of piecing together what had happened and in what condition he was at present.

He reached up and touched his jaw, which he found moving under its own power, and was shocked to find it intact. His ribs, too, seemed to have been knit back together by some mysterious magic beyond his comprehension. He'd felt them crack – he knew this. He had felt the intolerable lightning strike of broken bones in the depths of his chest. And yet, neither ripples nor jagged edges met his fingertips beneath his skin.

The only hint of any blunt trauma was a slight discoloration across his shoulder where he'd hit the ground, some sort of yellowish-orange residue covering a large section of his torso, and a dull ache in the hinge of his jaw.

Still in dismay, but nonetheless thankful for his good fortune, he became strikingly aware of several things. The first was that this was the first time in years he'd been fully sober, and the shock of his relative comfort in the face of such austerity was greater than his surprise at being alive.

Next were the brief, fleeting images of his recent passage in and out of consciousness which began in droves to return to him. He recalled the animals he'd seen, the tracks, the stench of urine, and in a moment of shocking clarity, he remembered his waking immobile, his staring up at the stars, and the impossible image of a man crouching close-by.

He looked around himself again, attempting to corroborate these fantastical experiences with the remnants of proof, but found the sand around him as smooth and undisturbed as the beach after a receding tide.

He had just begun chasing the specters of his memories when his body called him to attention. He was close to death from lack of water, and he needed to act. He hadn't endured this gruesome rebirth only to die of thirst in a desert 20 minutes from town.

But as he stood to walk, he suddenly knew he could not go back to that place, not for banishment, but because that town held the remnants of a life to which he had died and could never return.

So he turned instead to the west and set off at a tender pace with the morning sun on his back. In search of water, first and foremost, but also in search of something much greater. He was, for the first time in a very, very long time, in search of life itself.

As it does in the desert, the heat of the day came swiftly and without mercy. Without so much as a fast farewell, the chill that had hung on the stars was banished to the depths of the sandstone cliffs to the north, not to return again until nightfall.

Joseph wandered, looking for any sign of life, of water, straining his ears to hear the trickle of springs that were not there. In the month of May, one may be so fortunate as to find a rock-born spring here and there, clean enough to bathe and quench even the most delicate thirst, and sweet as honey. But in the heat of August, dried out from a summer's worth of torrential sunshine, the only sign of life to be found between the rocks down in the riverbeds were the winding tracks of desert lizards, or the brushstroke evidence of a long-gone snake.

But there were floods, and responsible for those floods were the monsoon rains which descended upon the desert quickly and departed with the same haste. When they came, they bathed the sands in life-giving abundance, but often not for very long.

Even then, the water that ran was no better than drinking the putrid downstream water used to wash the summer's sheep before shearing. In it one would find the dead and dying remnants of desert life, replete with mud and stones and sticks and salty dust scraped from the sunbaked rocks and dry riverbeds.

Once, when he was younger, he'd seen the monstrous, milkshake deluge pouring forth from a spout some hundred feet up the face of a cliff, and he'd been impressed by its tenacity. In many ways he already knew the dangers of the desert, having wandered long and hard through the barren hills and valleys, often half-dead from liquor and lack of sleep. But the truest danger of the desert – its implacable ability to strip a man of his ego and put him face to face with himself – this possibility he had never fathomed. Only now, sober and only tenuously alive, did he begin to confront that force of awakening.

Starved, dehydrated, and dressed in tattered shreds of bygone clothes, Joseph was experiencing the true majesty of this minimalist landscape for the first time. And though rather ungodly in his current state, he couldn't help but feel a new appreciation for what he could only describe as a sense of divinity welling up inside him.

He'd been wandering for hours and hadn't found anything worth drinking, so he decided to rest. Sitting down in the shade of an ancient juniper tree, he closed his eyes for a moment.

In a flash of vision lasting no longer than a split second, he saw a hawk drop from the heights and snatch a snake from its sunning place on some red rock surrounded by nothing but sand.

Startled by the clarity of what he'd seen, his eyes snapped open, and he found himself catching his breath. But he had understood the meaning of his vision to an extent that seemed improbable. Intuition was not something he'd ever understood, and he had, for his entire life until this point, preferred to take things at face-value.

But he'd seen the hawk dive and he'd seen the snake allow itself to be taken, and he understood two things. The first was that, in the desert, life always finds life. And the second was that all of life existed according to a natural order in which death was a fate, not to be avoided, but to surrender to when the time came.

The boy was surprised to find himself at peace with his place within this cycle, utterly accepting of his eventual death. But he felt that he now knew how to find water, because he had also understood that water is life, especially in these arid lands of sand and stone.

To find water, he had only to seek out other life among the harshness of his new surroundings and observe where it sought sustenance. Setting off again, this time with a renewed sense of peace and clarity and determination, he began to survey every detail of the landscape around him. He saw which way and from where the wind was blowing. He detected every animal imprint on the sand below him and took note from whence they came and to what destinations they could have been going.

He noticed the orientation of every modest plant and the slight variations in the coloring of the monumental rocks that comprised the canyon walls around him. He noticed the hanging gardens of the ferns held aloft in perpetual life by the eternal springs which seeped forth from the cool of sandstone. But those springs were consumed long before they became accessible to those confined to the ground.

He longed to live as a plant – if only for a time – content to subsist upon only sunlight and the providence of that life-giving elixir of mineral-rich waters.

But then he froze, for before him he saw a sure sign of salvation in the deep imprints of some large mammal. Perhaps made by a deer, or coyote, the careful footprints made no haste but surely, if followed for long enough, would reveal some source of viable water.

Any animal with enough weight to leave such deep depressions in the sand must surely require a legitimate water supply. Walking carefully so as not to lose his prey, but also out of respect for the benevolence of the desert, he followed the trail without the hurried panic of someone who is so close to death.

On numerous occasions, when tracks disappeared atop vast tables of solid stone that merged imperceptibly with the soft sandy ground underfoot, he had to search a broad area to rediscover them. But he did find them, without fail, and before much time had passed, found himself marveling at the animal's agility. Ahead, the journey up a narrow slot canyon was harrowing even for a nimble and able-bodied, though slightly emaciated, boy of twenty-three.

He climbed first on foot and then dropped to his hands and knees for stability. Along one side of his route the sandstone cliffs rose jarringly up to the heavens. Only a few inches to the other side, the ground gave way to an enormous and ever-growing expanse below.

The canyon itself was perhaps only ten feet across at its base, but that width grew gradually the higher he climbed. In several places he found he had to scramble straight up in order to once again catch the ledge across which his prey had travelled. The footprints had long since vanished, but something inside told him he was on the right track.

Why he must climb to find water, which usually travelled downward, perplexed him. But he understood that the desert, though capricious, is also loyal and owes no explanations for its ways. Life followed life, and life sought water. He was becoming part of that life, and part of that cycle, and part of that seeking. It felt purposeful to be a part of something larger than himself, no matter how vast or seemingly obscure.

After climbing for what felt like hours, the boy vaulted his tired frame over a ledge and found himself breathless, awestruck, and silent.

Before him, carved into the stone of the canyon wall, was a basin roughly four feet across, and only a foot deep in the middle. Seeping from the interior wall of the canyon ran a trickle of clear, sparkling water, feeding the shallow pool which shone like a diamond in the late-day sun.

Unsure as to whether the image before him was real or a figment of his hopeful, dehydrated imagination, he edged cautiously forward. Perhaps this was the work of some unkind destiny. Perhaps death had come and seduced him with the vision of the very thing he desired most in that moment. Water - life - lay before him, and he couldn't bear the disappointing possibility of it being a mirage.

He stared at the pool for a while, contemplating the miracle of this gift. Whether this image turned out to be real or imagined, he gave thanks for the opportunity of having arrived at life, or at death, to such a welcomed sight. A couple of times, he thought he could see Ellie's face shimmering on the surface of the pool, and in those fleeting moments he feared the whole thing may indeed be imaginary.

Finally he summoned his strength to face reality and, perhaps, to reconnect with it. Leaning forward, he reached out his hand and allowed his fingertips to dip just below the water's surface. He found it wet, and very much real. With a soaring excitement he began to accept that this pool before him was indeed manifest. A gift from God, or merely a gift from the desert - but was there a difference?

Slowly, his weary cognition lagging behind the hope in his heart, he allowed his whole arm to be lowered into the pool. He felt the bottom of the bowl and discovered it to be mesmerizingly smooth.

And then, as though he had been awakened from some trance, the reality of this opportunity – this invitation to continue living – hit him. Lifting his head to the vacant, deepest-blue sky above him he let out a howl of jubilation which served both to awaken the canyon around him and to shake him even further into his state of raucous celebration.

He nearly threw his whole body into the pool but thought better than to dirty the waters. Shoving his face under he felt life once again coursing through his veins. He drank slow and deep and before long, felt a sharp ache in his stomach from drinking too quickly.

Lying back, he reveled in the pain, each searing jab reminding him just how alive he was. His head throbbing, his stomach in knots, he fell into a fitful sleep on the edge of the pool. As he slept, he relived fleeting memories of his childhood.

But then, just before waking, the images suddenly vanished and before him he saw, once again, the same man who he thought he'd seen at his side in the days following the attack. Thick, black hair framed the angular face, and the man's eyes seemed to pierce the very fabric of reality. Again, he spoke not a word. The boy tried to ask him something but found himself likewise unable to speak.

Then, as suddenly as it had come on, the boy's sleep melted away into the haze and glare and sudden cool of evening in the desert. The sun had slipped below the canyon wall, and the sounds of the desert had changed. Crickets chirped and a gentle breeze was blowing through the canyon, rippling slightly the surface of the pool that lay unchanged by his side.

The boy found his body dripping from sweat that smelled strongly of unpleasant things and the breeze chilled him. More proof that I am alive, he thought, and he hustled to strip out of his wet clothes.

Lying down once more on another patch of stone still warm from the day's unrelenting sun, he felt a certain melancholy peace well up within him. The past and its pain were returning, and this troubled him. But he was also alive and awake and had found water in the desert. It felt to him as though from this point forward all things were possible, even acceptance, and moving beyond his wounds.

Feeling his lips, he began to assess his condition. But upon finding them still cracked and extremely tender, he decided pragmatism could wait until the following day. Lying there, naked atop the stone in the waning afternoon, he felt his heart soaring and a smile broke out across his face.

He was going to live.

The sun woke him as it kissed his chilled morning skin with warmth. He became awake very quickly with the change and he found himself stiff and hollow-feeling. How long had it been since he'd eaten? He wasn't sure, but certainly he was reaching the limits of his physical strength. In his stomach he felt a pit of emptiness, though he had discovered that he thought of food only occasionally and longed for it even less frequently.

Still, the part of him that desired to continue living more and more each day cried out with great urgency that something must be done to find sustenance. Surveying the canyon from his perch, he began to assess his options.

From where he stood, he could see the canyon bottom with its arid remnants of a spring-time riverbed. But aside from a few low-growing plants here and there and the occasional juniper, somehow still surviving, almost as an act of defiance, there was no life to be seen.

He sat down once again and urged his brain toward logical thought, though the lack of food made it difficult to reason. He had followed tracks to this place. Or rather tracks and intuition. Life discovers life. The hawk and the snake. Water and life are the same.

He saw the precariousness of his predicament, recognizing the absurdity of the challenge he faced. But he could not will the pieces of this puzzle to combine, revealing their solution.

As he leaned back against the rock wall he closed his eyes slightly. Again he saw the hawk dive and seize the snake from atop the rock, and again it startled him awake. Life discovers life. I am life, and I have found water. The thoughts trickled with agonizing sloth through his half-lucid mind.

He decided to splash some water on his face in hopes it would jar him slightly that he might function better. As he knelt over the smooth surface of the pool he saw reflected above him a hawk circling slowly, drifting in and out of view from his vantage point, and suddenly he realized:

If I am life, and this water is life, then surely other life will find this place as well. And then I need only to be ready to attack. With a furious excitement swelling within him, he jumped up and rapidly began making his way down the steep wall of the canyon towards a particular juniper which grew out of the fine silt in the dry riverbed.

In his moment of clarity, the thought occurred to him that he would need at least two different weapons, since he was likely to lose one off the edge of the cliff if he missed the first time.

Scouring the canyon floor, he found a sturdy branch long enough to serve as a spear. Not much further along he found a large chunk of sandstone that had broken off one of the cliffs above. Varnished and dreadfully sharp, it was large enough to inflict a fatal blow to the skull but small enough still to hold in one hand as he climbed up to his pool. Satisfied, he began to make his way back.

Much of his first day was spent grinding the end of the juniper branch against the sandstone to sharpen a point at one end. It was slow work, and his body tired easily. Every few minutes he stopped to rest, leaning back. On several occasions he fell asleep. By the time the sun began to flirt with the canyon wall to the west he had honed his weapons, and he felt sure that tomorrow he'd be given the opportunity to use them.

He slept that night more easily, though the hunger still gnawed at him even in his dreams. Bizarre and fantastical visions danced before him as he slept. Once, he woke suddenly to a sound, thinking the time had come, and that life had indeed found him. But, finding nothing upon waking, he dismissed the disturbance as wind or insect or...

Crickets! He had never eaten them, but he had heard of other places where they were considered a staple. He took a moment to weigh his options. The prospect of killing some sort of large game, then chopping it up without a knife, then either eating it raw or somehow finding a way to cook the meat... It seemed an arduous undertaking given his emaciated state.

In contrast, the thought of catching crickets seemed simple, easy. It didn't much matter anymore to the boy that he would be eating insects. Where the thought might have once repulsed him, he now found little difference between one source of food and another.

He considered, too, the reality that he may lay in wait, or even search actively, for some sort of prey for days before ever finding it. As hope for a proper hunt began to wane, he turned his attention back to the present.

Suddenly lucid and painfully aware of his hunger, he strained his ears to pinpoint the location of an especially loud cricket. When he thought he'd identified the direction of the sound, he gingerly crept toward it.

Raising his body ever-so-carefully over a small feature in the rock he saw it and sprang with a speed and agility that surprised even him. Peering beneath his cupped hands he found them empty. Perhaps it was darkness, or hunger. In any case, he thought little of it and listened again for another. Locating an especially loud chirp a little farther along the wall, he carefully made his way, as silently as possible, to the place from which it seemed to come. As he drew close, the sound ceased, and he shifted his focus to the little his eyes could see in the meager moonlight, and to what his intuition was telling him.

Finding a small fissure in the rock, he felt certain his prey lay just inside. As quick as a rabbit he placed his hand over the hole, but as he did, the cricket he sought jumped from another crack just above where he had placed his hand and disappeared into the blackness.

He sat down on the small ledge defeated. Perhaps it had been foolish to try. Perhaps he would meet a quiet death in this desert after all. But another chirp roused him from his gloom, and he mustered the courage to try just once more. Holding perfectly still this time, rather than seeking the sound, he discovered that perhaps the last cricket to get away had not gone far after all.

The thought surfaced in his mind that perhaps the desert was testing him, testing his tenacity and persistence. He wondered if this was some sort of hide and seek game he had entered into. He thought the stakes dreadfully high, for if he should lose, it could mean the end of his life.

But then again, he'd wagered that bet before, playing hide and seek with demons in bar rooms night after night.

And he had dared death to come take him each morning as he woke with bloodshot eyes and a terrible aching in his head. High stakes be damned, he thought.

Snapping back into focus he saw a glint of shiny black upon the sandstone just a few inches from him. A surreal concentration overtook him and he became animal, desert and moon. With a fierce explosion of muscle and an earnest growl, he lunged forward and seized the insect in his hands.

Before the cricket had a chance to jump it was being chomped between hungry teeth. Suddenly flooded with the energy of something living, his hunger piqued, and he began a manic search for more.

Throughout the small area he was willing to traverse under the veil of darkness he found only a few more insects, which disappointed him. But overpowering this disappointment was the ecstatic thrill of having found food.

As he sprang for a cricket perched close to the edge of the cliff face, he lost his balance and nearly fell a hundred feet to the base of the canyon. Shaking from adrenaline and the essence of life coursing through his veins, he managed to grab hold of the lip of a sandstone hueco and steady his body against the rock. Suddenly aware of the mere inches between himself and a very long fall he peered down at the darkness below and again he contemplated for a moment his earnest will to live in sharp contrast to his proximity to death.

But it hadn't scared him as he expected. Instead it stoked a flame within him that was still new to his experience, and it was the feeling of being alive. Edging back onto more stable rock he lay down. The cricket he had caught was still in his free hand, squirming to be let go.

As he lay back, his head dangling off the edge of the canyon wall, munching his catch, his eyes shone like sparks in the pale light of the moon hanging low in the sky. Satisfied and no longer quite so hungry, he decided that the following evening he'd descend the path to the canyon floor before darkness fell and catch as many crickets as he possibly could so that he wouldn't need to hunt the following day.

By this point, emptiness had become so familiar to him, that he preferred occasional spells of hunger to the monotony of constantly searching for his next meal.

Thinking better than to sleep half-way off a cliff, he began to move to a more secure position. Besides, his neck was beginning to get stiff, and he was growing tired as his body began, for the first time in over a week, to digest once more. Eventually, sleep found him, and this time he did not dream.

It was already mid-morning before he rose the next day, and the sun beating down was uncomfortably hot. After washing his face and hands and drinking his fill of the crystal-clear water from the pool, he began to make his way down.

The hunger he felt upon waking delivered the reality that he most likely couldn't subsist on crickets alone, and the sun above urged him to find some other way to spend his day than lying around.

Reaching the bottom of his trail, his spear in hand, he set out towards the mouth of the canyon. Looking back, he made a mental note of this particular location so he would be sure to find his way back later in the day. The meager sustenance of the previous night's spoils had awakened in him a curiosity and ambition that had eluded him for a very long time. Once again, he felt like a child, eager to explore every inch of his temporary home.

All day he wandered through the brush of the open desert, occasionally stopping to rest under the shade of a juniper.

By mid-afternoon he was beginning once again to feel dehydrated and knew he should make his way back before long. He hadn't traveled far but had rather spent much time in examining every plant, every imprint in the sand.

It was as though the desert had become his lover and he was eager to experience every inch of her. With great joy and the gentlest of hands he caressed the curves of the ancient trees which grew where nothing else would. With great interest and attentiveness, he followed the contours of canyons from where he stood at their genesis.

Once or twice he caught sight of a shadow racing across the ground and looked skyward quickly enough to catch a glimpse of a hawk or a buzzard surveying the land from above. These sights gave him great solace, and he began to associate these large birds with omens of good fortune and prosperity and he smiled upon seeing them.

Strange, he thought, that this desert, which for many defines the inhospitable, should now offer me so much comfort.

As he meandered back towards his canyon, he came across a new type of tracks the likes of which he had not yet encountered. There, deeply imprinted in the crusted sand, were the clear pints of horse hooves. Just one animal it seemed, which meant someone had passed this way. But the tracks led across his path and not down it.

Shaken from his blissful solitude, he suddenly longed to follow them, to once again find a small outpost, or perhaps even a town, and to begin to explore this new life he had discovered amidst the rocks and sand.

But the sun hung low in the sky and his thirst urged him to seek water. He didn't know how long he would need to walk before finding anything, or even if the tracks would end up taking him anywhere. Against the whims of his heart, he made note of the location of the tracks and continued on towards his canyon, and beyond it, his pool. He could always come back tomorrow.

On his way, he stopped to snatch a few crickets, something he found easier with every catch. The improvement pleased him, and he walked without much thought given to his surroundings.

As he heaved himself over the last step up to his plateau he froze. Not but four feet from him stood a small doe, suddenly startled by his appearance over the ledge and pinned in fright against the back wall. As the boy was positioned directly in front of her only path of escape, her options for flight were extremely limited.

They stayed like that for a long time, each staring into the eyes of the other, each willing the other to move first, Joseph caught almost in a trance at experiencing first-hand the deliverance of the desert.

Slowly, he reached for his spear. Except for crickets, he had never hunted before, and he didn't know whether he could do it. Sensing his hesitation, the doe broke her statued stance and bolted for the path down the cliff. Jumping clear over him, she landed with thundering hooves on the sandstone mere inches from where he stood and ran with impressive speed down the precarious path towards safety and the ground below.

Stunned and awed, he stayed in his spot on the ledge for some time, marveling at her. As he watched her bound down the near-vertical flow of sandstone he couldn't help but feel that nature had afforded greater grace and agility to deer than to men. But I still have my thoughts, he thought to himself. Who knows if does can wonder?

It seemed every day, every new experience, introduced to him a new level of exhilaration. Each new image he saw, or scent he smelled, or miracle he discovered; each new thing enlivened him even more.

It's amazing what life has to offer if you look for it, he thought. Or maybe all it takes is to stop clenching your eyes shut.

Something roused him the following morning before dawn had broken, and he was grateful to catch the last of the dusky dark before daybreak. Early pre-dawn morning held a stillness difficult to explain. He knew that today he would set off in pursuit of whoever had made the tracks he'd found the previous day. Somehow he knew he would not be returning to this place.

As he marched onward through the fading dark and out of the mouth of his canyon, he allowed himself to forget the face of the walls, the scent of the juniper and the character of the canyon's edges. Some things are better left to mystery, he thought to himself. His thoughts surprised him.

It wasn't long before he once again picked up the horse trail of the previous day and began to follow it. The tracks wound in and out of sagebrush and eventually out of the canyon lands in which he'd spent the last several days. As he made his way to the flatlands, he found himself confronted with an open sky more dazzling than he could ever remember seeing.

The first light of dawn was creeping over the horizon while the last stars still hung in the cerulean sky. Silhouettes of cactus and juniper stood stark against the breathtaking backdrop as a scarlet ribbon of sun appeared to rise from the desert itself.

How long it had been since his eyes had been clear enough to see, his mind sharp enough to appreciate a sunrise. Here, a familiar scene met him, but it was with new eyes that he experienced it. In his old life, the only time he'd seen the sunrise had been when he was still up, and almost always still drunk from the night before. In those times, he cursed the sun and its rising, wishing that the bleak, feigned death of darkness would remain forever. But this was a different dawn, and he welcomed it.

He knelt there in the sand before a small patch of rabbitbrush, buds held tight in anticipation of their autumnal blooming. He considered the buds, and smelled of their early honey scent, and he realized how good it was to be alive and to be awake. Really awake, and not drowning. And he thought to himself that he never wanted to run like that again.

My father ran, he told himself. My father ran and it hurt me. And his father ran, and that probably hurt him. But I'm not going to run, he told himself. I'm not going to run and I'm not going to hurt anyone by running.

Though it might be painful, he realized he would rather face his past in his full strength so that he could be finished with it once and for all. No more forgetting. No more hiding. No more running.

A faint breeze tousled his hair and he felt heard and understood and like there was something bigger than himself that was there supporting him. A smile broke

across his face and he stood, the morning sun casting a
golden hue across the desert before him.

Part 2

He had been walking for several days before he came to the edge of what appeared to be a modest village. It was nestled at the base of a mountain range and seemed to be mostly small houses with livestock scattered about the surrounding land. Here and there a young boy or girl tended to chickens or cows, but beyond that he saw few people.

He came to discover that, in spite of his rather mangled appearance no one paid him much mind. I guess people in this area are used to strange men emerging from the desert looking half dead, he thought to himself with wry amusement.

As he passed a glass window in one of the buildings nearer to the center of the village he caught sight of himself. Rather gaunt from a diet of crickets and severely parched, his reflection startled him. He wondered how none of those he'd passed since entering the sparsely inhabited farmland around the town had seemed surprised by his appearance.

Turning slowly to get a good look at this face in the reflection, he took stock of his state. His clothes were beyond mending, his hair in knots and caked with red sand. His face bore a scruff he hadn't known he could grow, and his jaw looked slightly crooked.

He recalled the night of his attack when he'd tasted blood just before passing out and gave thanks that a crooked face was all he had to show for it. As he looked once more into the glass, his gaze rested on the eyes of the man looking back at him. Within them he perceived a spark that had not been there before. There was a certain fire inside his heart. As he stood admiring his own eyes in the reflection, he saw someone move just beyond the glass and an instant later it slid open.

From within the building, a face peered out at him. It was a girl, not more than twenty, and startlingly beautiful. In the depths of her eyes, Joseph detected both excitement and gentleness. She stared without smiling, and for a moment he could neither think nor move. There they stood for what felt like a small eternity, locked in each other's near-expressionless gaze.

Coming back into himself he began to fear she might think he had been peeping in on her. But as he began to try to explain, her face broke into a broad grin. At once he felt his heart melt.

"What are you doing here?" she asked, but her tone was not threatening. "You look to be in rather rough shape..."

Joseph paused, the stillness of the desert slowly returning to him. In her voice there had been a kind reassurance and he immediately began to relax.

Her eyebrows betrayed her curiosity at the image of this boy before her, looking as though he hadn't slept under a roof in all his life, and this made him feel both emboldened and a bit embarrassed.

"I'm a traveler." he told her.

"Well by the looks of it, not a very good one." She smirked.

"On the contrary, my lady," he said. "You see, I've just been talking with the desert, and we had a bit of a disagreement as to whether I should live or die."

"Well by all means! What was the outcome?" she asked, playfully animated and now leaning a bit out the window, resting her chin on her hands.

"We compromised and decided I should keep living. But there was one condition: I did have to die first. What's your name?"

"I'm Margaret, but most call me Mary. And yours? If you're allowed to tell me... I'm not sure of the rules. I've never conversed with someone who has just died." She laughed, her voice like tinkling bells, and her whole posture encouraged him to give her more. But at that moment someone hollered from farther up the road.

"That's my brother. You'd better go. He may not be as generous as the desert. Meet me back here tonight when the moon is high."

With that, Joseph ran off towards the town he could just barely see in the distance. Once or twice he looked over his shoulder, curious to see if he had been followed, or at least watched as he retreated. But all he saw was the man – Mary's brother, apparently – and Mary speaking in the doorway of the house.

Once he reached the outskirts of the town proper, he slowed to a walk and began to take in the busy world of humans once more.

For the first time he was struck by the pains people would go to in order to feel comfortable. He saw workers erecting a new building, sweat streaming down their tanned necks in the mid-day heat. Across the road, men argued about something or other, and further down still another struggled to coax his draft animals up onto the platform to be loaded onto the train.

In contrast to the peaceful serenity of the desert, the town was very loud. The steam from the train engine hissed as men and women and children hollered at each other through the streets. Horses whinnied and chains clanked and doors slammed here and there. The sensory intensity made Joseph's head spin.

As he walked, he thought of the austerity of the desert and of how effortless life had seemed there. Or perhaps it wasn't that life had been effortless, but the effort required was always momentary and immediately rewarding. I'll bet that man with the animals is already thinking about what he'll purchase when he sells that team to the buyer down the line, Joseph thought to himself. And the men building that storefront surely are not the ones who will use it, his thoughts continued. How complicated and absent this world seems after only a short time away in the wilderness.

Passing a small store that seemed to sell food goods, he decided to stop in to see if he could work for the store owner in exchange for something to eat. When he stepped through the door, every conversation in the room stopped at once. Through a mixture of disgust and surprise, the eyes of everyone in the building fell upon him.

Ignoring them, Joseph walked boldly to the counter and asked the shop owner if there was some cleaning he could do in exchange for some bread. With a face betraying no emotion at all, the shop owner stared hard at the boy.

One of the men on the customer's side of the counter with lifeless eyes, his cheeks and nose bloodshot, said loudly, "How about you start with yourself," which elicited a laugh from the others in the store.

Undeterred, Joseph held the eye contact of the shop owner. The man who'd spoken up went back to his conversation, and gradually the rest of the occupants did the same.

After what felt like a long while, the shop owner responded, quietly and discretely, saying "I cannot have you working for me in that condition. Go and get yourself washed up. Comb or cut the knots from your hair, and get yourself a shave. Come back tomorrow at sunrise and I'll find something for you to do."

Still hungry and a touch discouraged, Joseph returned to the street and set his mind to work determining how he would manage to achieve the impossible. How could he shave with no blade? Untangle his hair with neither brush nor comb? And even if he could, how could he possibly bathe when there seemed to be no water in the area?

As he walked toward the edge of town, as much in search of solutions as to escape the noise, a boy a bit younger than himself ran up from behind. For a brief instant Joseph's mind flashed back to his attack that night in a town not unlike this one. He felt the adrenaline rise through his body, his hands tensing into fists, his subconscious jerking to attention in anticipation of attack.

He was prepared for a fight before he was fully aware of what exactly was happening, but turning quickly, he saw the boy meant no harm. In fact, across his face was a grin that immediately set Joseph's heart at ease.

The boy explained how he'd overheard the conversation in the shop and wanted to help him. He handed him a small burlap bundle containing a straight razor and some soap. He hadn't been able to find a comb, but assured Joseph that the soap would work wonders on his hair.

"It's Sister Anna's secret recipe, made with goat's milk."

Joseph thanked him for the gift and the assistance. The boy stood and rocked back and forth on the balls of his feet, seeming hesitant to leave.

"Do you have anything to eat?" Joseph asked. The boy shook his head and his eyes fell to gazing at his feet. He appeared embarrassed to not have anything to offer.

Feeling ashamed of himself for making such a bold request of someone who had already been so kind, Joseph changed course.

"What's your name?" he asked, hoping he could lighten the conversation.

"Gabriel, at least that's what Sister Anna calls me. My mother called me Dante," answered the boy.

Joseph began to wonder who Sister Anna was.

"Do you know where I might find a stream to bathe in?" Joseph asked, thinking it miraculously convenient that Gabriel – or Dante – had appeared right at this particular moment. He was in an unfamiliar town and in an unfamiliar condition of spirit, and though he had not often held many close relationships, there was no doubt that a companion could make things easier for him. It would help with the loneliness, too.

"Yes!" Gabriel answered, and seemed overjoyed to be able to help.

The two made their way towards the mountains to the east and after a short while came to a spring which, in spite of the time of year, ran clear and hearty.

Gabriel sat down at the base of a nearby tree and began to whittle a stick, seeming content to pass his time as his new friend tended to his appearance. As he took the knife from his pocket, it caught Joseph's eye. For reasons he couldn't explain, he felt as though he'd seen it somewhere before. Its elegant bone handle, its swooping blade engraved with someone's initials... He couldn't place it, yet it seemed intimately familiar.

Before Joseph could even undress, a muted, far-off bell was heard from the town and Gabriel jumped up, explaining that he had to get back to Sister Anna, and that he hoped he'd see Joseph soon.

Glad to have some privacy, and to be with the quiet of the mountain stream, Joseph looked after Gabriel as he left. The boy ran with such lightness in his feet. There was something about his presence that made him immediately likable.

But Joseph was weary, and there was work to be done. He finished stripping off his ragged clothes and piled them haphazardly on the bank. He unrolled the burlap bundle given him by his new friend and placed it near the water's edge.

He eased in slowly. The cool water felt heavenly on his hot, dry skin. It felt right to bathe here, in this running water, ever fresh and surrounded by such lush greenery. On the banks of the stream were all manner of low-growing groundcover plants and the soil was rich and loamy.

How strange to be in this place when only this morning I was walking out of the desert, he thought to himself as he began to ceremoniously splash water over his shoulders. Joseph watched as the current swept away the dirt and sweat and struggle from his skin.

As he ran his hands over his ribcage, he again marveled at the fact that nothing seemed to be broken. In post-traumatic recollection, he tasted the metallic blood on his lips, felt the sting of cracking bones and smelled the smoke of the tavern he'd left – been thrown out of – only moments before.

What would've happened, he wondered, if I had not been thrown out that night? What would've happened if I hadn't been walking with eyes closed? What if I hadn't gone that way, and hadn't been attacked? If I had not died that night and come back a new man, would I even be alive today? And actually, if that mysterious man I saw in the firelight had not found me and somehow healed me before disappearing back into the desert, would I have survived? Or rather become food for the desert itself, consumed by flies and buzzards and other scavengers?

As his thoughts played out the numerous coincidences that had led him to this time and place, he found himself awash in gratitude at the way things had turned out. Looking over to the burlap cloth laid out on the riverbank, he reached for the soap.

He decided to make his washing a sacred act, and as he ran the soap and cleansing water over each bone and muscle, he gave thanks to his body for carrying him into life – carrying him through life – even when he himself had not been sure it was worth living.

Around him the late summer afternoon seemed almost a dream. Through the trees poured golden sunlight, the leaves adding their filtered glow and the water reflecting silver flecks such that the entire forest seemed to be dancing.

He lay back in the water to wet his hair and rinse his body, and as his ears went under, a deep peace filled him. Water. How he loved the way it caressed his skin and danced in whispering delight through his hair. Patiently, and with great care, he began to work the soap through his tangles, and as Gabriel had promised, the knots gradually began to work themselves out between diligent fingers.

He stayed in the river for some time but decided not to shave. He had no mirror and was unsure he would be able to shave his crooked jaw without cutting himself. Mary would be surprised to see him so clean, and maybe she wouldn't mind his scruff. After all, he thought, she didn't seem to mind it when I turned up looking half dead this morning.

When he had had his fill of the river, he drew himself out of the water and lay down atop a mossy bank in a beam of sunlight. Completely at ease, he closed his eyes and allowed the birdsongs and wind through the treetops to overwhelm the hunger in his stomach. Before long, he drifted off to sleep and found himself again dreaming of Ellie.

In his dream, he was in the middle of a vast expanse of very fine sand. The wind whipped dust devils and threw eroded debris mercilessly against his face. Still, forward he trudged. Behind him he pulled a sled laden with old possessions he'd had at various times in his life.

Beside him, Ellie walked, seeming to grow ever more discontent. A few times he tried to strike up a conversation with her, but his mouth seemed unable to speak words, and so he gave up. Gradually she began to walk faster, and for a while he tried to keep up, or to take her hand, but whenever he did, he would lose his grip on the sled poles and would have to stop to regain his hold.

Eventually she was so far ahead he could hardly see her. He stopped walking and watched as she vanished into the swirling sand. In the dream, he was about to collapse, overcome with grief and defeat, when a noise and something wet and cold roused him. He found himself on the mossy bank, though the day's sun had all but set and a twilight had descended around him. He had slept away what was left of the afternoon.

At his head was the curios muzzle of a dog, sniffing this human who lay sleeping in the woods. It jumped back, tail between its legs, when Joseph moved. Easing up to a sitting position, he spoke softly to the animal, noticing that its ribs were visible and its body cowered.

"It's okay boy, don't worry. I'm no threat to you. If I had some food to give, I'd share. Hey, have you ever tried crickets? Not too tasty, but they've got a nice crunch."

As he spoke, the dog seemed to relax and eventually sat down to watch him from a safe distance. Through the trees to the east, Joseph saw that the moon had already begun to rise through the cooling twilight. He thought of Mary and realized that if he were to meet her as she had requested, he'd better get moving.

He bid the dog farewell and, after gathering his things and once again dressing in his tattered clothing, began to walk back towards town. A few times he glanced behind, and noticed the dog following, never coming too close, but never losing sight of him either.

The dark grew long around him and, as he walked, he was grateful for a full moon to light his way. He passed the silver-shadowed silhouettes of buildings and strolled unhurriedly through the town center, walking in the middle of the road.

Around him, townsfolk went about their evening affairs. It was not yet very late and there were still many people out. A few glanced in his direction – his tattered clothes made him stand out – though he thought he looked considerably better now, after his bath.

A few times, he stopped, enchanted by the image of a family at a dining table through a glass windowpane, or by the beckoning comfort of a candle-lit hearth in some house or another.

He thought of his youth and missed the familiarity of home, even though that same home had been such a painful place. As he walked, he wondered if he'd ever find such comforts again.

Before long he had passed through the town and was again coming to the outskirts, returning to the desert, and drawing closer to Mary. The thought of seeing her again made his heart a little lighter. It also made him curious.

What did he have to offer her? He was poor, wounded, and unkempt with no home and no job. He wondered for an instant if it was a trap. After all, he didn't know her very well – or really at all. But what could she steal? Chuckling to himself, he thought it humorous that the very fact of his poverty, which had previously made him feel insecure, was now a reassurance. He continued on, focusing his attention on the beautiful night through which he now ambled.

After a time he came to the edge of the small village in which he'd first met her. His mind coursed over what he'd say to her, and he began to grow a bit nervous, though not from fear. It was just the way thinking of her made him feel in his chest.

As he drew nearer to her house – or at least he thought it was her house; everything looked different in the moonlight and he began to doubt even his memory of the place – he heard a loud whisper from a small barn to his right.

"Hey! In here!" she called, and her voice was sweeter than the wind through the trees in the forest.

Before he could reach for the handle, the door swung open and he was met with darkness inside.

"Come in!" she said, and her voice betrayed her own excitement.

He walked in and the door shut behind him. It took a long moment before his eyes began to adjust, and still he struggled to see.

Looking around him in the darkness, he saw Mary standing just inside the door, nearly close enough to touch him. Next to her was a basket filled with what appeared to be some sort of cloth, and next to that was a lantern. He saw no others in the barn – not even animals – though it smelled strongly of fresh cut hay.

After a few moments of silence he saw – or perhaps felt – Mary draw herself close to him and press her body against his, landing a kiss on his cheek. "I'm happy to see you," she said simply, and set herself to lighting the small lantern.

At once the room was filled with a soft light and he noticed she'd been careful to drape a heavy blanket over the only window so as not to give away their location.

For the first time since that morning he really saw her. She was even more beautiful than he remembered. Perhaps it was the lantern light, or the cloak she wore, or the ribbon in her hair, but she seemed older than the girl he'd met in the window.

He stared long and hard into her eyes, and she stared back, not the least bit startled, and without a shred of modesty. Her lips curled slightly at their edges, but otherwise she looked on with a confidence beyond her years.

"I've brought you some things." Mary said, breaking the dance between their eyes.

Joseph began to interrupt to tell her it wasn't necessary, that she shouldn't have, but she kissed his mouth only briefly and giggled when it stopped him speaking at once.

Removing the folded fabric from the top of her basket, which he now realized were men's clothes, she removed a half a loaf of bread and some strips of dried meat. Handing them to him, she explained how her family had continued to dry most of their meat, even though there had been new developments which allowed for meat to be kept fresh for more than a single day.

Joseph ate heartily, expressing his gratitude through mouthfuls of food. Mary just smiled and waited patiently as he ate. Several times he offered to share, feeling embarrassed to eat alone in front of a woman, but each time she politely declined and reiterated that this was for him, that he should eat his fill.

Once he had finished, which didn't take very long at all, he drank from a bucket in the barn and sat down on the ground. Mary came to him and knelt by his side, running her hand over the scruff on his chin. "I rather like the look of a rugged man." She told him.

He smiled warmly at her approval but explained that his boss the following day expected him to show up clean-shaven.

He told of how he'd been given a razor that afternoon but had been nervous to shave without a mirror. Mary asked if he'd brought the razor with him and offered to shave his face. She explained how she'd learned to shave a man's face by helping her grandfather to prepare for church each Sunday, since his hands shook too much to be able to shave himself. Each week since she was just a girl she'd helped him and had become quite adept at the task.

Humbled by her offer, he accepted, and they made ready their make-shift barber's station. Amidst the hay and dark of the barn she found the milking stool and sat him down upon it. Hanging the lantern on a post nearby she brought over the water bucket.

Working the soap from his bundle into a thick lather, she spread it on his cheeks, chin and neck. Then with expert grace and the utmost care, she drew the blade over his skin.

He couldn't say for certain that he'd ever been cared for in such a tender manner, and he found himself deeply relaxed. All the anxiety about seeing her again had melted away. Thoughts of Ellie had vanished. Even the memories of his youth seemed held at bay by the loving touch of this woman.

A few times he dared to watch her work, moving his eyes as she walked from side to side, admiring her execution as she looked for any missed spots. She pretended not to notice his gaze but secretly hoped he would never stop looking at her. When she was done, she walked to her basket and returned with a handkerchief.

"I'd intended to give this to you, but I think it'll be better used to clean you up."

Carefully, Mary wiped the soap from his face and dried the droplets of water which had fallen on his collar bone. "Okay, take off your clothes."

He was surprised by her demand, and even more so by the confidence and matter-of-fact tone in her voice. "Take off my clothes?"

"Yes, I've brought you some clothes I borrowed from my brother, but I need to make sure they fit you."

He began to strip. He'd expected Mary to turn around, or at least divert her eyes, but she stood before him and looked on as though he were merely sweeping the floor. Slightly embarrassed, but not wanting her to know, he proceeded with a feigned confidence.

Once he'd stripped to his undergarments, Mary stood for a moment, taking him in. But her face told of neither disgust nor disappointment nor desire. She was like a sculptor assessing her own work, determining the next cut to make, the next feature to shape.

After what felt to Joseph like an eternity she turned and walked to the basket, retrieving the clothes she'd brought. "My brother is a little bigger, but I think these will work." she said. Walking up until she was just inches from him, she handed him the clothes, and gave him another kiss on the cheek. She lingered. He smiled.

Joseph put on the clothes, and though they were indeed a little large for his frame, he felt like a new man in these wares that were not torn to shreds. "I'll bring them back as soon as I can buy some of my own," Joseph said.

But Mary refused, saying they were his to keep, and it would be better not to return them since her brother might then realize they had been missing in the first place.

They began to converse. Mary implored him to tell of his travels, of his past, and though he talked liberally about his time in the desert, he realized he had no desire to tell her about his old life. Those stories are no longer a part of who I am today, he reasoned, so there's no sense in telling of them here.

As he spoke, Mary watched his lips hungrily, but Joseph didn't notice. He was adrift upon the stories he spun of his last few days, his mind back among the stone and sun of the arid plain that had delivered him into this new life.

He was in the middle of telling her about his encounter with the deer at his desert pool when she suddenly lunged at him and landed a generous kiss right on his lips. The force of her advance knocked him back and she landed atop of him.

Again she had transformed from a simple, generous, and curious girl to a determined, self-assured woman who was prepared to take what she wanted. For the first time he allowed his hands to hold her, and he kissed her back. Her lips were the softest thing he'd ever felt, and they awakened in him such a passion that he could not help but pull her face to his by the nape of her neck.

His whole body was on fire and the only thing keeping him from floating away on a whisp of smoke was her delicate body holding him against the ground. How can a woman be at once as light as a feather and as heavy as the weight of lifetimes of love, he thought to himself?

He felt love and life course through his body, and he realized how much he had wanted her. Perhaps this was love, he thought, and he surrendered to the pressure of her hips and legs as they straddled his torso, her hands around his face and her lips locked to his. He surrendered to her hands which searched eagerly for his skin, and to the pure unencumbered pleasure of the moment.

He woke to the sound of a door latch and jumped to his feet in alarm. But realizing where he was, and seeing no person enter the barn, he walked to the small window and looked out just as Mary rounded the corner of the house a few hundred yards away.

He looked around as his eyes readjusted to the dim light of the early morning. He knew he needed to get moving if he was to meet the shop keeper at dawn as he'd been instructed.

Feeling more confident than he had the previous day, he walked to town with a skip in his step and a smile on his face. The coming sun offered a whispering warmth that hinted at a hot day ahead, and Joseph said a little prayer of thanks for another day to live.

He arrived just as the shopkeeper was sliding the key into the lock on the front door. It took him a moment to recognize the boy for he looked so much different than the vagrant who had come seeking work the day before.

"I didn't think I'd see you here this morning."

"Well, here I am. And I'm ready to work."

The shopkeeper nodded as he opened the door.

He first tasked the boy with sweeping the shop and the boardwalk out front. Stepping outside, broom in hand, Joseph was grateful to have the opportunity to be outside as the dawn was breaking over the mountains to the east. The birds chirped their daybreak songs, the town roused slowly from its night of sleep and at seven o'clock, the bell in the town center tolled once for each hour of the morning.

Just as he was finishing his sweeping he noticed a man walking towards him and recognized him at once as the man who'd chided him about his appearance the day before.

As though he didn't recognize Joseph at all – for indeed he didn't – the man walked past and, with a tip of his hat, entered the shop, immediately striking up a conversation with the shopkeeper. Some people never recognize what's right in front of them, Joseph thought to himself.

When he had finished his task, he returned to the shop to be assigned his next. The shopkeeper put him to dusting the shelves in the back that held the sacks of grain.

This proved to be tedious, filthy work. Great clouds of dust billowed each time a grain sack was moved, causing him to choke. Joseph remembered the handkerchief from Mary which was still in the pocket of his pants, and he tied it around his face as a mask.

It seemed as though the job could never really be completed because of all the dust in the air that was sure to land back on the shelf as soon as it had been cleaned. He paused to think. If he could knock the flour from the sacks outside, and then clean the empty shelves...

One by one, he brought each grain sack out back and brushed it off so that most of the dust on the outside was carried away on the wind. By the time he came back in with the final sack, the dust in the air had cleared and he was able to go to work on the shelves.

He asked the shopkeeper for a bucket of water and a few rags. In this way, he could clean the shelves without launching clouds of dust back into the air. While he worked, he thought constantly of Mary and the night before. The way she'd looked at him as though she'd known him forever. The way she'd shaved him as though he were the only man in her life.

Did that woman know no strangers? Had she been a figment of his imagination? No, he knew her lips had been real. He'd felt her on top of him, had allowed her to kiss him with all her eagerness and joy. Replaying their evening over and over in his mind helped the time pass more quickly.

Before the noon hour, he had completed the task and the room shone with clean shelves and neatly stacked grain sacks.

Joseph returned an empty bucket with the wrung-out rags hung neatly on its edge. The shopkeeper peered into the back. He hadn't expected the boy to finish this task at all, much less before the noon hour. He grunted and nodded his approval and asked the boy to join him for the noontime meal. His home was close by, and his wife was fixing fried salt pork and sweet potatoes. As they walked, it was the shopkeeper who broke the silence.

"You clean up pretty good for a wanderin' fella."

His accent was more heavily southern than Joseph had realized. The boy started to talk about how Gabriel had overheard the conversation and had come to his rescue, but decided instead to say only that a friend had lent him some things with which to clean himself.

"Well, I guess it don't much matter how you get it done, long as you get it done in the end."

Joseph appreciated the man's ability to accept what was without too much thought. When they arrived at the shopkeeper's house, he was surprised to find the man's wife waiting out front for them. He wondered if somehow he'd been caught for his escapade the previous night.

Was this woman a friend of Mary's family? Had someone seen him leave the barn that morning? His thoughts began to race, his mind coming up with every possible explanation for how he'd come to the place and how he'd come by these clothes.

But as they drew near enough to make out her face, he discovered to his immense relief that she was smiling, her eyes dazzling with admiration for the simple, stoic man she called her husband.

"She's always waitin' on me when I come home for dinner." And though his voice seemed deadpan flat, there was a sparkle in the man's eyes and the corners of his mouth twisted up in the hint of a sheepish grin. The shopkeeper walked by her with a smile and a tip of his hat and went inside. With Joseph a short distance behind, the shopkeeper's wife waited until he drew closer, then she held out her hand.

"I'm Elizabeth. You must be the boy Samuel was talking about this morning."

"Joseph, ma'am. Pleased to meet you."

Elizabeth exuded sweetness. She had green eyes and long blonde hair that curled a little as it fell on her shoulders, and her smile was warm and comforting. After a moment, he caught himself staring at her, and lowered his gaze. She giggled. She likely wasn't much older than Mary, maybe his own age. Blushing a little, she changed the subject. "Goodness, how rude of me. Come on in and sit yourself down."

Joseph ducked in through the front door, noticing it was shorter than normal doors. Once inside, his eyes adjusted to the dim interior and he took stock of his environment. Along the back wall stood a cast iron kitchen stove and a farmhouse sink big enough to bathe in. Along the wall were shelves holding plates, glasses, pots and pans.

There was a worktable in the middle with a thick, pine top and big, sturdy legs. The walls, too, were clad in pine with an aged silver sheen indicating that some of the boards had been salvaged from previous buildings.

Elizabeth went about serving them as they sat at the table and sipped some coffee. "I bet Sam hasn't said but two words to you all day."

The shopkeeper smiled and winked at her, and she smirked back at him.

"Well, I'll consider myself lucky then. I'm certain he's said at least twice that many."

Elizabeth laughed. "You're in much better condition than Sam told me. He made it sound like you'd just crawled out of a swamp."

"I don't think I was that generous," Sam said, swirling the coffee grounds in his cup.

Elizabeth swatted at him with her dish towel with an "Oh you stop it." As they ate, she asked the boy about his life and his family. When his response about the latter was brief, she didn't push the subject. They talked of how much the town had grown, what trouble the rail line had brought in, how folks were always worried they'd run out of water soon. Joseph complimented the food and thanked Elizabeth repeatedly for the meal and hospitality.

When they'd all finished eating and the boy had had two generous servings, Elizabeth got up and cleared the table, returning with a small cloth bundle containing another two servings of pork and a few biscuits from that morning. He thought to object, thinking her kindness too much, but decided instead to just express his modest thanks and accept her generosity.

"You come back now any time; you hear me?"

"Yes ma'am, I cannot thank you enough. You have been so kind to me. I will remember it always."

As they walked back to the shop, neither man spoke. They were both full and drowsy from the heavy meal, even in spite of the coffee. It was now early afternoon and the shop began to pick up a little.

Sam had asked Joseph to work on restocking and taking inventory of some of the hardware flats behind the counter. He was busy counting out a bag of bolts when a woman's voice made him freeze where he stood. He didn't need to turn around to recognize her. But it took him a minute to know how to react.

"Good afternoon, sir. I'm looking to buy some hardware for a door latch on our barn."

"Yes ma'am. Of course. Joe here will be happy to help you with that." As he said it, Sam clapped him on the back.

His hands were shaking from nerves and he nearly dropped the bolts he was counting. Slowly he turned, trying his hardest to compose himself, though he was sure everyone in the room could see how off-center he'd become.

Mary stood there on the other side of the counter, looking like an angel. And Joseph stood behind it, completely lost for words, his cheeks flaming. Should he pretend he didn't know her? Should he make known that they knew each other?

She seemed to be alone. Perhaps there was no reason to be alarmed. Still his palms were sweating and his thoughts raced.

Mary seemed unflustered. Actually she seemed to be enjoying herself. She stood leaning slightly to one side, her arm through the handle of a basket and her hand on her hip. A knowing smile spread across her face as she stared intently. Joseph knew he had to act.

"What sort of latch is it, Ma'am?"

"Oh, well you should know..." She smiled again and his stomach dropped to his knees.

"I... I should?" he stammered.

"Well yes, of course. A capable-looking young man like you must surely know a thing or two about barns. Don't they all have the same sort of latch?"

Relieved, he was able to catch his breath. Sam looked on in amusement at the exchange but seemed content to let it play out without his interference.

"Of course," he said. "Yes, these should do the trick. How many do you need?" He counted out the pieces and placed them in a small paper bag. Mary thanked him for his assistance and winked as she walked out the front door.

Joseph stood for a moment, shell shocked, before Sam chuckled and said, half under his breath, "If I didn't know any better I'd say that Margaret Lane has taken a liking to a certain young store clerk."

Joseph stared expressionless, and Sam chuckled again.

"Now lighten up. She's just a woman. You're some young fella. Heck, even Elizabeth seemed to like you. Anyway, I'm just about outa work for you today. Why don't you come back tomorrow and I'll have you help me put up some new shelves I've been meaning to get to. It'll be a whole lot easier with an extra set of hands."

Joseph agreed enthusiastically and thanked him for the work and the meal. Sam pulled a dollar out of the register and handed it to him, and Joseph thanked him again.

It was still early afternoon and there were hours of daylight remaining. He thought of going back to the stream but didn't want to wash Mary's smell from his body, so he decided instead to explore the town a little.

After all, now he had a job and some clean clothes, and he could easily blend in, passing as a regular townsman. He enjoyed his feigned invisibility and as he walked, marveled at the ease with which life seemed to be unfolding around him.

Coming to the center of town he found a bench and sat down. Opposite him, across the town square, was the tall bell tower which tolled every hour. There was a small plaza between the tower and himself and a few young children ran about playing with a hoop they'd managed to pull off a barrel.

The afternoon sun was warm and pleasant, and it seemed the coming autumn had already begun to take the edge off the heat. He was lost in thought, watching the children play, when from the corner of his eye he saw a figure approach from his right.

Before he saw her fully, he was intoxicated by her smell, and visions of the previous night came flooding back to him. He turned just as she sat down. Mary had positioned herself close enough that their flanks and shoulders touched, and this public display of proximity and familiarity made Joseph slightly uncomfortable. Still, he didn't move away and neither did she.

"I've been wandering this town all day waiting for you to appear," she said. "When I caught sight of you in Sam's store I nearly jumped up and down."

"You could have given us away, the way you acted in there," he said.

"Oh calm down," Mary insisted. "There's nothing wrong with a little harmless flirting. Besides, pretty girls are good for business." She laid her head on his shoulder. He was surprised by this action, but it brought him such joy that he simply smiled a little as he continued to gaze across at the clock tower.

"When will you come visit me again?"

"Aren't we together now?" he asked.

"I mean when we can be alone. When I can fall asleep on your chest and dream to the sound of your breathing."

"Don't you worry that we'll be found out?"

"No - everyone in my house is too concerned with themselves to notice what I'm doing. Except Mother, but she knows and thinks it's wonderful that I've finally taken an interest in a man. She's always fussing about me becoming a spinster and dying alone."

Joseph chuckled. "Surely there must be boys in this town who fancy you?" he wondered aloud.

"Of course. But I don't like them. They're all so plain. So safe. So flat and predictable and horrendously boring.

And rude. When you blew in on the wind looking like you'd lost a fight with the desert itself, I couldn't believe my eyes.

"In your face was the struggle to live, and the determination to fight for your right to keep struggling. You were thirsty for life itself more than you were thirsty for water."

"Certainly, when we met I was not in the best condition. But here I am now, clean and shaven, a man with a job in a store, and somehow you still want me. I'm just as boring as the rest of them."

"You may be clean and proper – or more proper – on the outside, but in your crooked jaw and in your eyes like sparks I still see the dance of the desert fire, the sun rising and setting, the moon casting its glow over mountain streams. In your blood runs the wild and I cannot take my eyes off of you."

The bell tolled marking five o'clock and Mary cut herself short.

"Goodness, time has gotten away from me. Look what you do to me! I must be going. Please come to me tonight? I won't sleep a wink without you."

She kissed his cheek and trotted off in the direction of home, the golden light of the August afternoon painting her effortless curls in gilded hues, her dress flowing behind her. Once she had crossed the plaza, she turned back and, catching his gaze, smiled before disappearing down a side street.

Joseph continued to sit, basking in the glow of young love and late summer. The sun was catching the hands of the clock on the tower, and he noticed for the first time how intricately beautiful it was.

He was tracing the contours of the dark blue glasswork behind its hands when he was again joined on the bench, this time by Gabriel. Joseph wondered, somewhat perplexed, if he had somehow sat in the center of the world.

"It's a beautiful clock isn't it?" Gabriel said, more as a statement than a question.

"Gabriel, I cannot thank you enough for the blade and soap."

"It's nothing! I've been helped by unseen hands. It is the least I can do to help a stranger. Although you're hardly a stranger anymore. But look at your clothes! Where did you get them?"

"It doesn't matter. What's important is that I now have a friend in this city that's still so new to me!"

"Well, you look better than you did yesterday, so I'd say whatever you're doing, you're doing it right." Gabriel grinned broadly, and again Joseph noticed how much he felt drawn to this boy.

"Would you like to know the legend – and it's true; I know because Sister Anna told me – of this clock? I'll tell you." Gabriel crossed one leg over the other and placed his hands on his knee like some grandfather about to recount old war stories or cowboy tales. Joseph wondered if this was the pose taken by whomever had relayed this tale to Gabriel.

"A hundred years ago there was a man who had traveled from Italy to find a new life in the still-new country of America. He decided the time had come for something new. Really he came to get away from all the fighting.

"He stowed away on a ship bound for Boston. Then he crossed the entire country, always in search of the perfect place to build his greatest work. He was a well-known clockmaker in his own land. He traveled thousands of miles by horse, by mule, and even on foot. He carried with him a small bundle of tools which he had inherited from his grandfather.

"When he arrived in this town, which at the time was barely even a settlement, he took one look at the mountains and he fell in love. He also found, upon arriving, that most people here spoke Spanish. Spanish, I'm told, is very similar to Italian, and he had learned some of the language as a boy.

"So he set himself to finding the money to build his masterwork, and he just happened to find it in a good-hearted town mayor. He wasn't really the mayor – it was called something different, but the job was the same.

"So he worked for seven years, traveling hundreds of miles in search of the best materials, all the while being paid only a pittance. Three years into his project he met a woman who loved his hands and his spirit. They had a child together, whom they named Stella. He also took on an apprentice named Niklaus, a loyal young man with a sharp intellect, who had also emigrated from Europe. He worked day and night, and eventually came to the final stages of his beautiful clock, the crown jewel of his life's work.

"But just as he was about to place the hands on the clock face, a support of his scaffolding gave way and he tumbled to his death.

"He was just moments away from finishing his masterwork, and God or someone decided at that moment that his time on earth had come to an end. Some say that if he were to have completed the project, he would have felt a great emptiness inside himself. They say that perhaps it was necessary that he should die before finishing."

Joseph was mesmerized by the story, and when Gabriel paused, his wide-eyed gaze moved from the clock to the boy. Gabriel continued.

"Of course, Niklaus completed the project in honor of his dear friend and teacher, and dedicated the clock to Stella.

"Niklaus taught Stella all he had learned about the art and craft of building clocks, and she became a promising student. Eventually, Niklaus began to grow old. Stella took over the shop and began to teach her own daughter, Anna.

"But Anna had no interest in clocks and wanted instead to become a nun, and so at age fifteen she left home to live with the sisters in a monastery, almost fifty miles away. There she learned to live a pious life and devoted herself fully to Christ.

"One night, she had a dream in which an angel of God spoke to her and told her to return to her home and continue the legacy of her grandfather. She was to meet a young boy who was in need of a mother, and she was to care for him as though he were her own.

"So, she came back to her hometown and, shortly after returning, she met me. She didn't like the name I was given by my birth mother, so she named me Gabriel after the angel who appeared in her dream."

Joseph stared in amazement. "Are you telling me that your late, great-grandfather built this clock?"

A look of pride spread over Gabriel's face. "Well, no. My own great-grandfather was a bastard and a drunk who's only legacy and gift to the world was dying early. But Anna's grandfather – the man who is in many ways responsible for my being here today – built it."

"Gabriel, that's amazing! I would like to meet Sister Anna. She gave me soap, and in many ways gave me a friend – you. I'm eager to thank her."

"Of course!" Gabriel exclaimed. "In fact, where are you sleeping? I'm sure we could make a bed for you in my room. Unless you already have a place?"

Joseph paused, smiling as he considered how things in his life seemed to be so effortlessly falling into place. Then he answered, "I would very much like to stay with you, Gabriel. But not if it's too much of a burden. I've managed on my own for years and I'm not afraid to do it again."

"Don't be ridiculous. I'll ask Sister Anna tonight and meet you here tomorrow. Perhaps you'll join us for supper then?"

They bid each other farewell as the clock tolled. Once again Joseph was left on the bench alone. His stomach rumbled and he remembered the pork and biscuits Elizabeth had given him earlier that day. As he ate, the sun began to approach the horizon to the west, and he looked on in wonder at the watercolor sky.

His thoughts drifted back to Ellie, to the opportunities he must have passed up during his years of drunken avoidance. He remembered his dream of pulling the sled through the desert. He thought of the fierce and fearless love Mary expressed, even though they'd known each other little more than a day. He thought back to those nights in the desert where he had indeed faced death and somehow managed to convince God – and himself – that he was worth one more chance.

Briefly he recalled the face of the man who had tended his wounds – surely that's what must have happened... he would not be alive under any other circumstances.

Elizabeth's cooking lent him a warmth and solace he'd forgotten during his chapter of desert austerity. His body was adjusting to food and water and true nourishment, and the food sat heavy in his stomach, making him drowsy. Or maybe it was the feeling of belonging, of things working out, of ease. Every step toward normalcy lent another layer of comfort, peace, and serenity.

Feeling content, he rose from his bench just as the sky was beginning to darken, and as he walked, he listened to the sound of the crickets. He noticed that the cricket songs now reassured him that no matter where he went, and no matter what he encountered, he would always survive. He felt in-tune with the world, fluent in its language, and he was proud.

The walk to Mary's went by quickly and she nearly knocked him to the ground in an aggressive hug as soon as he walked through the door of the barn.

He was waiting at the shop the next morning when Sam arrived. The man smiled and tipped his hat as he approached, and the two set to work as though they'd been partners for years.

They talked more that morning than they had the entire first day, in part because they worked side by side hanging the new shelves, but also because Sam had grown more comfortable with the stranger. He had his own share of wild stories to tell, and the two got on like old friends. By the time they arrived at Sam's house for the mid-day meal, Elizabeth could barely get a word in.

"I've never seen my husband so talkative. You two must be cut from the same cloth."

They just smiled at her.

That afternoon, Sam showed Joseph how to work the cash register, handle the hoist out back and spit sunflower seeds into a bucket across the room. Joseph showed Sam a few card tricks he'd learned in the bars.

For a while, Sam had him work the counter while he took a short nap. This charge made Joseph feel immensely confident, and he felt even better that each customer who came in during his shift left satisfied and smiling.

At five in the evening, the bell tolled signaling closing time. Sam told Joseph to take the next two days off and return on Monday, to which he agreed. He was paid another dollar and sent on his way.

Joseph was happy. He felt at peace, grounded in himself while enjoying all the fruits of his sober life. He began to try to count the months and years he'd wasted in a drunken haze but gave it up quickly because it began to depress him. Without meaning to he had again come to the plaza, but before he could sit down, Gabriel ran up to him excitedly.

"Joseph! I talked to Sister Anna and she would like to invite you for supper! I hope you can join us! You can see her clockmakers shop, and have some of her famous cooking, and tell us both all about your travels."

He was surprised and excited to see the boy, and even more excited by the dinner invitation. After hearing the story of the clock tower, and the lineage in which Gabriel had somehow become entwined, the enigma that was Sister Anna enchanted Joseph immensely.

He accepted at once. The young Gabriel grinned wholly and then ran off, shouting over his shoulder that he'd tell Sister Anna the good news, and that Joseph was to meet him in the square in one hour.

With nowhere else to be, Joseph again assumed his now-usual seat on the bench across from the clock tower. A few pigeons pecked around and a few stray chickens joined them. But besides the birds and the occasional person walking from place to place, the square was empty. He thought it odd that the town could be so dull on such a beautiful Friday evening, but appreciated the quiet and solitude nonetheless.

He hadn't seen Mary all day and for a moment he wondered about her. But it was less of a longing and more of a passing curiosity and he allowed it to take him drifting into a fantasy. He imagined walking up to the front door of her parents' home, a bouquet in-hand, and knocking boldly upon the wooden planks. When they answered the door he'd stand tall and proud and tell them he'd come to ask their daughter's hand in marriage.

He paused, his dream interrupted by logic. I've only just met this girl, he thought to himself. Isn't it too soon to be dreaming of spending the rest of my life with her? Do all boys dream of such things? And do I even desire marriage to begin with? He found himself confronted with a conundrum, but decided to circumvent its hazards instead of exploring them. He pushed the thoughts aside.

He again imagined standing at her front door, a look of judgement and surprise upon her father's face, a subdued excitement on her mother's. He stood his ground in the silence as he awaited their answer.

After an impossibly long pause, they invited the boy to come in and sit so they could talk things over. As he entered the home he noticed Mary looking on from the doorway nearly out of sight. Upon her face was the thrill of love, and he smiled a greeting in her direction.

Her father asked the usual questions, wanting to know about the boy's employment, his own family, his debts, his qualifications. Her mother was silent, beaming at Joseph. But then her father asked a question to which Joseph found he did not have an answer. "And why do you want to marry? What good would a marriage do for a young, unencumbered boy such as yourself?"

Again shaken from his daydream, this time by a question asked of him by a figment of his own imagination, he frowned. *What is marriage? What is commitment? Why do I desire to marry? Toward what end does this bring me?*

The questions swirled in his head and drove him to a discontentment he hadn't known since before his rebirth in the desert. He knew he desired a partner, but for what purpose he was not sure, and this irritated him. He decided his were good questions to ask of Sam and Elizabeth. They seemed perfectly happy together, and after all, Sam wasn't much older than himself.

Still troubled by the interruption to the ease with which his life had been carrying on, he stared blankly ahead. In a melancholy daze he watched the birds and stared past the few pedestrians walking across the plaza. The sun began to set, and before he knew it, Gabriel was walking up to take him to dinner. Upon approaching, Gabriel immediately recognized the glum look on his friend's face and asked what was the matter.

"Why do we love?"

The younger boy was confused, and asked what Joseph meant.

"I mean, why do we love? Why do we seek to find love, and then seek to hold it in the bonds of something so permanent as marriage? What is it about a woman that can make a man abandon his entire life in order to stay in one place with her?"

Gabriel was silent as they walked slowly across the square, his brow furrowed in contemplation. His friend's question was a silly one. *We love because it's our nature,* the younger boy thought, but he said nothing as Joseph continued speaking.

"Did you know, I once heard a story of a boy not unlike ourselves who was crossing the desert in search of a treasure, and he nearly gave it all up for a woman. And at the end of that story, after finding his treasure, he went right back to her. The boy had never dreamed of living in the desert, but he went for love. It seems crazy to me. I cannot figure it out. So I ask again, why do we love?"

Gabriel stopped and turned to his friend, his body blocking the path on which they were walking. He placed his hands upon Joseph's shoulders and looked at him. For the first time Joseph realized how lively and dark his friend's eyes were. Behind them danced a wildness he hadn't noticed.

"You're overthinking this. I've learned that there are some things we are not meant to know. It's better not to chase after them before they're ready to be caught. When we do, we sometimes become so desperate to catch the idea that we grab onto something else instead. Then we end up getting the whole thing wrong. We make our own truth and when the real truth reveals itself to us, we don't believe it."

He released him and continued to walk. Joseph was dumbfounded. It was as though a higher power had entered the boy and spoken directly through him.

But the confrontation had done the trick, and once again Joseph returned to his joyful self, less concerned with the greater picture and more content to live each moment in its own time. Gabriel had shaken his shoulders and in the process dislodged the conundrum that had taken Joseph away from himself. It's good to have a friend, he thought to himself. And maybe love and friendship are not so different. So he let it go.

Gabriel was already a few paces ahead by the time Joseph once again regained his composure, and he ran to catch up.

Just past the edge of the little town they came to a stone cottage with a wooden barn situated immediately to the south. A stone path wound its way to the front door, lined with flowers standing tall against the summer's heat. The door stood open slightly.

"Here we are!" Gabriel exclaimed as he brushed some dust off of Joseph's clothes.

Joseph was about to ask if there were any bits of information that were important to know about Sister Anna when the door opened the rest of the way and there appeared an Italian-looking woman wearing a light blue apron and her hair in two braided buns on the sides of her head.

"Welcome! Gabriel has told me a little about you, but I'm quite excited to learn more about the boy who blew in with the wind!"

She seemed angelic in manner and smiled constantly. The corners of her eyes were wrinkled, hinting at decades of happiness, and her cheeks were rosy and plump. Just being around the woman made Joseph happy. As though she'd known him for years, she took him by the shoulders and kissed him once on each cheek.

Joseph expressed his gratitude for the invitation, and they stepped inside the cottage. Once he had passed through the door he felt himself transported to another world – an old one, set in a painting of an Italian cottage he'd seen once. Braided garlic hung from the exposed wooden rafters, fresh ingredients were scattered across the stone countertops, and plates and dishes and cups lined open shelves on the walls.

The room was simple, but each thing present was well cared-for and tidy, and a delightful scent filled his nose. Anna bade him sit and poured him a little wine. Joseph was taken aback, and paused before speaking. This had been the first time since his decision to quit drinking that alcohol had been offered to him, and he found himself unsure of how to proceed.

He also realized this was only the first of many times he would be required to advocate for something important to himself at the expense of insulting someone's hospitality. He didn't want to seem rude, and considered pretending to drink it, but felt it would be better to be honest.

"Thank you, but I actually don't drink..."

She gave him a surprised but understanding look and replaced the glass with one filled with water, smiling as she put it on the table.

"How silly of me – I should have asked first!" she said, a warm but bashful look in her eye.

"I appreciate your hospitality. In another time, I did drink, too much in fact, and in the desert I saw that something needed to change. I think in a lot of ways I died, and was reborn with a fresh opportunity to live. I couldn't squander such a second chance."

He stopped speaking and realized the others had also stopped what they were doing. Both Sister Anna and Gabriel stared fixedly at him. He wished he hadn't said so much.

A short silence followed, broken eventually by Anna, who was once again smiling broadly. "I am grateful you are here. Second chances are a gift, and I am humbled by your gratitude and awareness."

As she spoke about second chances, she glanced at Gabriel with the same twinkling eyes and warm smile, and he reciprocated, nodding a little as she spoke.

"First, we will eat, and then I will show you around. How does that sound?"

Joseph agreed enthusiastically, feeling more at home in this strange, unfamiliar cottage than he ever had in his entire childhood. He recalled how, just two nights before, he'd walked to meet Mary, stopping occasionally to peer in at the families around their tables, eating and carrying on. Now, in what seemed the blink of an eye, it was he who sat at the table, and his own heart that was filled to bursting with feelings of acceptance and love.

As they ate, Anna told of her youth, of her grandfather, of the convent in which she'd become a nun, of meeting Gabriel. They shared their thoughts on love and God and the power of the desert. Gabriel spoke a little of his own youth and Joseph found himself admiring the boy for his tenacity and strength in spite of a childhood which had been, if his stories were to be believed, even more tumultuous and trying than Joseph's own.

He found that he felt a kinship with the boy since both of them had been the victim of all the terrible things alcohol can do to a man, especially when that man is a father to a young boy. Gabriel had had it worse. But there were things between them that they both knew because of what they'd seen.

He also discovered Sister Anna to be a wise, patient, and generous soul. She viewed the service of others – and the giving of second chances – to be her sacred duty in life, and she took it seriously.

"Still, though my purpose may be to love, my work is to continue the lineage of my family, working with my hands, and building clocks. Don't ask me why – I don't know. But an angel of the lord told me, and so I don't ask questions."

The door to the cottage had remained propped open after they entered, and the light and sounds and haze of early evening had filtered in throughout their conversation, the light of the setting sun shining brightly through the door and landing on the table at which they sat. This sunlight gave the house a dreamy glare and painted Sister Anna's rosy cheeks in a joyful hue.

The meal was delicious, and filling. Joseph stuffed his stomach as full as he could of the wonderful food until he could hardly bear to think of eating another bite.

After a time, Anna told the boys to follow her. Leaving her apron on the table, she led them out the front door, down the path and to the small barn just next to the house. Outside, a goat munched on some hay, tethered to one corner of the building.

"That's Affamata. It means *hungry* in Italian. She's not stopped eating for even a single instant since I got her seven years ago. At first I thought it was because she was just a kid, but eventually I accepted that she was fully-grown and would spend the rest of her days eating from dawn to dusk."

Anna swung open the door to the barn and stepped inside; the boys followed. As his eyes adjusted to the dim light of the barn, which like Mary's, had only one, north-facing window, he could hardly believe what he saw. Against one long wall of the barn was an enormous work bench set before hundreds of drawers ranging in size from barely an inch square to well over two feet in width. In one section, there were no drawers but rather a large peg board holding all manner of intricate tools.

Though the floor was dirt, not a speck of dust could be found on anything above the floor, and to one end of the work bench were a few objects standing up on end covered in what appeared to be velvet cloths.

"Please, have a look around! It's not much fun if you just gawk from a distance!"

Of course this was nothing new for Gabriel, so he stood by Sister Anna and watched his friend discover this world of enchantment. But Joseph was lost. Beside himself with wonder and amazement, he felt once again that he'd been transported into a whole new world.

Tracing his fingers over the well-worn workbench, following the contours of every immaculate drawer face, looking over the many tools hung up and on various shelves, he eventually came to rest staring at an enormous, gilded clock hand, intricately forged with detailed finery all along its length. It was trimmed with a glossy black edge and seemed destined for some masterpiece of a clock.

"That's an exact replica of the hand of the clock that my grandfather was placing when he died. It was commissioned by the mayor after the clock tower had been completed, and Niklaus crafted it himself. However upon delivery, the mayor handed it back to him with a letter, which read that the hand was intended as a gift for the craftsman's family; a way to share his immense gratitude and condolences, along with a check for the full amount of the commissioned hand times two."

There seems to be no end to the litany of goodness woven throughout this family, Joseph thought to himself.

"Gabriel tells me that you currently do not have a place to stay."

Joseph was shaken from his trance by Sister Anna's words, and he turned slowly, allowing his mind a few seconds to make sense of what she'd just said.

"This is true, though I've lived for a long time on my own, and I don't want to impose. I'm happy to bed down by a stream or in some field."

"Silly boy, winter will be here soon. And then where will you sleep?"

"I've always managed to find something suitable," he said with a smile. "I've found the human body much hardier than you might expect."

"Well that may be true," Sister Anna responded, and for a moment she paused. "But would it not be better to have a safe and warm place to stay when you like?"

"Yes, certainly," he answered. "It's just that I would hate to burden anyone who would show such generosity."

"Well then, I suppose we'll have to put you to work in the shop so you can earn your keep."

Joseph smiled. Thoughts of hours spent in this place, in the company of this woman, flashed through his mind and a warmth suffused him. Regaining his composure, he put up one last fight.

"But won't it be a burden to find work for me? Surely with such a fine young man as Gabriel all the chores and tasks are well-tended to?"

"My boy, hush. You underestimate the toil of this shop and our small farm.

"And you overestimate this boy's work ethic," she added with a chuckle, prodding Gabriel in the ribs with her elbow. He smiled sheepishly.

"Well I would be a fool to decline such hospitality. But I have to be honest. I know nothing of clocks, and even less about caring for animals. And the second I become a burden you have to promise to kick me out."

Sister Anna reassured him that his brilliant mind and zest for life were qualification enough for the position and the lodging, and she promised to oust him the moment he became a nuisance.

"Come, let me show you to your room."

Joseph looked to Gabriel, surprised that one had already been prepared. His friend just smiled.

The room was small, and the bed smaller still, but it was certainly more comfortable than a sandstone slab, and much safer than a dry riverbed.

Gabriel's was the next room over, a bit larger, but just as modest: a straw mattress spread across a rope-strung cedar frame next to a small, hand-hewn stool that served as a nightstand; and a bible. Both rooms had small glass windows set deep into the stone walls, and a mirror hung on the wall across from a very small, framed picture of Jesus. The dim light from the late autumn evening cast a meager, dreamlike light over the room. Joseph set himself down on the bed and took a deep breath.

Was it possible that he had indeed died in the desert, and that this was some sort of beautiful afterlife? But he caught himself, and remembering what Gabriel had said earlier, decided not to think about it too much. Whether life or paradise, he had to acknowledge that this second chance he'd been given was nothing short of miraculous. He felt a warm gratitude emanate from his chest as he gazed out the window at the twilight. Crickets chirped and a slight breeze blew, rustling the leaves of one of the citrus trees in the yard.

Another sigh. He was growing tired. He ventured out to see if he could help Sister Anna with the cleaning, but she shooed him out of the kitchen with her broom and told him to rest, and to look forward to fresh eggs and goat milk biscuits in the morning. So he rested. He wouldn't wake until breakfast time the next morning.

In the weeks that followed, Joseph's life became quite busy. He worked most days at the store, and spent his afternoons, evenings and weekends helping at Sister Anna's. He tried on several occasions to pay her for his room and board, but each time she refused and scurried away before he could insist. So instead of giving her the money, he set it aside to give to her when the time came for him to leave.

If he left it on his bed when he left, he reasoned, she'd have no choice but to accept it, because by the time she found it he'd be long gone. He didn't realize as he had these thoughts, but there was a piece of him already that knew he wouldn't stay in this town for long.

He continued to see Mary every few days, but it grew harder and harder to make the time, since his commitments made his free hours scarce. She was bothered by this and he could tell, but she said nothing, growing sulky instead. Joseph left the topic alone. Still, she remained the wild child he'd met that day in the window, and frequently came into the store while he was working just to see how much she had to do before he became distracted by her presence.

Each time she did this, Sam looked on in amusement and chuckled. And each time, she'd leave before Joseph had a chance to speak with her, because he was always helping other customers.

In stark contrast to his increasingly sparse relationship with Mary, his friendship with Gabriel had grown quite deep. The two boys talked for hours, never finding the end of their shared interests. Beyond their chores, they frequently stayed up late on the nights Joseph was not with Mary, talking and playing cards.

For the most part, Joseph came and went as he pleased. He knew which chores were his responsibility, both around the farm and in the workshop, and he always saw to it that they were completed. Sister Anna never commented on his habit of being gone all night several times per week. He wondered if she noticed. He assumed she must, because Gabriel always did, and he knew Gabriel noticed, because he always commented.

He learned to milk and care for the goats, how to tend and butcher chickens and ducks, and how to churn butter. He learned, too, how to cook, and how to mend simple clocks, and began to learn some of the craft that Sister Anna had inherited from her grandfather, and his friend and assistant, Niklaus.

He heard stories about the venerated men, and about the fierce and independent Stella, who had wholeheartedly encouraged Anna to abandon her family trade to pursue her calling at the convent.

As he became more and more a part of their lives, he grew to feel an ever-increasing fascination with, and admiration for, their history.

One day in late December, Joseph had been dismissed from the store a few hours early due to an especially slow afternoon. It was the first time in several months that he left the store with nothing immediately requiring his attention. Mary wasn't expecting him, nor were Anna and Gabriel.

He decided to walk for a while and explore the town he'd come to call home but still knew very little about. He knew well the square, and the paths from Anna's home to the store, and his route to Mary's. Even his path to the creek at the foot of the mountains where Gabriel had brought him to bathe on his first day had become familiar, because he often went there to pray or be alone for a while.

But the side streets, the alleys, and the various quarters that made up the town as a whole remained largely unknown to him.

So on this blustery and grey December day he walked. For a while he wandered, turning where he wouldn't normally, and allowing the fast-dying afternoon light to guide him. He ventured down narrow streets, stepped in some places to accommodate the steep grade, and lined with hanging pots which in the spring and autumn months had held brightly colored flowers. On this day, though, they hung empty, and a chill in the air whispered half-empty promises of snow.

As he turned onto a wider avenue, he found himself approaching a fenced lot on which the house had been built toward the back. The house differed from those on either side of it not only in its proximity to the street, but also in its architecture.

Most houses in this part of town were constructed of felled logs or adobe, but this one was planked in vertical cedar boards which had been painted white with a shake shingle roof and two large windows facing the street. A bright red door was positioned evenly between them. Everything about the house transfixed him.

In the ample plot which stood before the house, he could see fallow rows that he assumed grew a host of garden plants - or perhaps flowers - during the warm season. Beside them, and in every corner, stood the wilted, dead stalks and leaves of various plants. Whoever lived here had clearly dedicated a great deal of effort to this masterpiece of a garden.

And how curious the house was! It was as though it had been picked up from some eastern prairie town and placed here in this desert settlement by accident.

As he stood and looked on, studying every detail of this enigma before him, he began to wonder what other mysteries lay throughout the parts of town he'd never bothered to explore. He resolved to walk a new path each day that he might unearth more of this town's hidden secrets.

He was interrupted in his thoughts by a woman approaching from his left, her features obscured by the low sun which was setting almost directly behind her and a hooded cloak she wore against the cold. In fact, he couldn't clearly see her until she was immediately before him, and he was startled to find that she was young and quite beautiful. She smiled as she passed him and unlatched the gate to the yard, and then without looking back, she strolled up the path and unlocked the door.

Joseph collected himself and called out. "What's your name?"

She paused, looking over her shoulder in mid-stride.

"Madeline."

"Is this your garden?" he managed to stammer. His heart was pounding inside his chest and he found it difficult to breathe.

She nodded, smiling, and went inside, closing the door behind her. As she disappeared, she looked back once more, and they locked eyes for the briefest moment. Her gaze seared into his memory.

She seemed like a woman out of another time, her hair falling freely on her shoulders in a cascade of glossy brown. And her hands – her hands had been so nimble and so effortlessly controlled in the way they maneuvered the gate latch.

He was flustered, speechless and immobile. He stood for a while before a horse cart passed by and roused him from his fixation.

Shaking his head, he walked on, but he saw nothing else for the rest of his afternoon, for all he could remember was that brief instant when she had glanced back at him as she entered the house, and the way she had smiled almost imperceptibly.

He was walking aimlessly down another side street when he was tackled from behind by Mary.

"I've been looking everywhere for you! And oh my, is something wrong? You look like something is wrong; your eyes are very far away. What happened? You can talk to me, Joseph."

Joseph again shook his head, trying to get his jumbled thoughts back in order, but in the end he decided to reply to her with a smile and a kiss on the forehead.

She took his hand and they walked together for a while, her keeping hold of his arm with her free hand and huddling into him for warmth and for comfort. As they began to pass through a busier, more familiar part of town she stopped walking abruptly.

"There's something I need to talk to you about."

Joseph was surprised and paused, turning around to face her. He asked what was the matter. He wondered for a moment if she'd grown tired of his busyness and was going to end things. He didn't have a reason beyond intuition to think this, but still the thought occurred to him.

"I would like for you to meet my family. We've been going for several months now, and I think it's time you met my mother and father so they know where I've been spending so much time." Her eyes twinkled as she spoke, and her face bore a smile, but still in the tone of her voice he detected a searching and a longing and a plea that he might show her he hadn't completely left her behind.

Joseph was about to reply – was about to try to explain that he wished to continue as they were, and to not complicate things further, and that he was so busy at the moment with his commitments to Sam and to Sister Anna, and a whole host of other things – when he remembered something he'd heard in a story once.

It was that love is better felt and not spoken of, and that talking about it with the one you love only ever makes it more complicated and less pure. He didn't know this to be true for himself, but it certainly felt as though anything he could say to Mary might only make things worse.

So instead of speaking, he walked the few steps back towards Mary, took her in his arms and kissed her. He gazed into her eyes and told her that he was so glad she'd found him on that side street. And then he kissed her again and took her in his hem and continued on.

They continued walking, both feeling content to share the space between them, to be close to one another in the cold, and to venture forth with very little defined at all.

Still, she wondered why he seemed so distant, while he himself wondered how he could come to know more about that mysterious woman in the little white house with the red door. But they each pretended not to notice and walked on in silence.

Joseph and Sister Anna had grown quite close, and she had taught him a great deal about her family's craft, about wood and metalwork, and about living a good life. He now routinely carried out more and more specialized tasks for her, and she always looked upon his progress with pride.

Gabriel, too, admired Joseph's natural talent, and sometimes even asked him to share his methods that he might learn something new.

One morning in April, as the boys were cleaning the goat stalls in the barn, the two of them were talking and working. It was a cool morning but it would be a hot day and the sun was climbing fast through a very clear sky. Outside the birds chirped and some of the citrus trees were starting to bloom and the smells of their flowers flowed in on the breeze and made it a very nice day for working. Gabriel took a sharp turn in the conversation.

"I've noticed it's been a while since you stayed away for the night. Are things okay between you and Mary?"

Joseph danced around the subject, but Gabriel was insistent.

"I'm not one to judge, but you seem different; troubled. The spark in your eyes has faded... Except for some days when you return a little later than normal, always coming from a direction that isn't toward Mary's house, and isn't toward the store. On those days you're on fire. There's an angst in your face and I can tell you're dissatisfied. It's like you're wishing for something that isn't there."

Joseph paused, stopping his work for a moment, and leaned on his rake, looking pensive. After a while, he answered, "There is a house on a very small street. I don't know what it's called. It is unlike any house I've ever seen before, and the land it's on is equally strange. There are rows and rows of garden, and the shoots have already started to come up, and the flowers have all begun to bloom again."

Gabriel looked confused. "It sounds like a great place... But... a house? All this is because of a house?"

"It's not the house," Joseph responded shortly. Whenever he thought of that house or of Madeline he became agitated. He hadn't realized the effect it had on him until this moment. Gabriel's face betrayed his surprise at his friend's hot-tempered response. Minding his tone, Joseph continued.

"The house is owned and cared for by a girl – no, a woman – who's now taken over every thought in my mind. All I know about her is her name, but I still can't stop thinking about her."

"Maybe you just want what you can't have?" Gabriel asked, trying to be helpful. He was also feeling bad for Mary that Joseph had become interested in another woman.

"No, it's not that. I don't even want her!" Joseph retorted. "But whether I want her or not, she is there in my mind when I walk or when I eat or when I sleep. It's beyond my control! I don't want her, but I'm consumed by everything she represents, and I can't even explain what that is."

"I think it's normal to find new people intriguing..." Gabriel offered unconvincingly, becoming ever more confused.

"Ugh! You don't understand! She's not like us. She smiles and the clouds clap in thunder. Her eyes flash in my direction and I see the history of the world in which men fought and died for the love of a woman like her. She is the Madonna, the divine incarnate."

Gabriel found his friend offputtingly dramatic. "Everyone is just a human. You're building her up into something holy and you don't even know her. Have you talked to Mary about all this?" he asked cautiously.

"Of course not. Mary is always worried about losing me and obsessing over our time together. I've tried to explain that I'm just busy, and that I spend as much time with her as I can. There's no pleasing her! So if I were to tell her about any woman – much less this woman who seems to occupy every free thought in my mind – I'm sure she would come undone."

"But don't you think she can sense your distance, and maybe that's why she's looking for reassurance?"

"Maybe." Joseph frowned. He wasn't enjoying this conversation.

Gabriel forged ahead in spite of his friend's clear disdain. "And what about you? You don't owe Mary anything. You're under no obligation to love or satisfy her. You're not married to her. Sister Anna has told me over and over to honor that voice inside of me which speaks truth. She reminds me to follow my heart, just as she did when she felt her calling to join the nuns at the convent; just as her grandfather did when he left his home country to come here."

Joseph was still frowning, but he listened nonetheless, his gaze fixed on the younger boy. Gabriel continued.

"To me, and this is just my observation, it sounds like you are no longer in love with Mary, whether because of this new woman or not. The most honorable thing to do is to tell her so.

"You owe her the truth. It's the only right thing to do."

A silence settled between them. Joseph's frown had deepened, and his brow was furrowed.

Gabriel took note and said nothing more on the subject. Nevertheless, he recognized a need within his friend and thought he could offer support another way.

"It seems you have some things you need to get clear on. Why don't you go for a walk to the stream and see if you can find what you're looking for? Maybe you just need a little space from all this." His tone sounded genuine.

Joseph thanked him, set his rake to hang on its nail on the barn wall, and walked out into the warm spring day.

Above him, birds fluttered back and forth, and the morning sun shone boldly upon the fresh shoots of crocus and hyacinth which grew along edges of the flagstone path from Anna's barn to the road. Stepping outside seemed to immediately cheer him, or at least release some of the tightness in his brow.

With each step, he knew with more and more certainty that what he was feeling needed to be worked out. That it would destroy him slowly if he continued to ignore it. His conversation with Gabriel had brought up a host of uncomfortable truths he'd been trying to avoid. The time had come to face these things.

Beneath his feet, the ground was soft, supple and fertile. The spring thaw was in full effect, and he could hear the trickle of snowmelt under a dense cover of fallen leaves throughout the forest.

Here and there a tree snapped, the warming wood imitating animal sounds, but he paid little mind. Though Joseph had initially relished the opportunity to feel his life once more after years of alcohol's sedation, he was finding it harder and harder to bear the weight of the sorrow and complication that love seemed to bring.

How many people drink because they don't know how to love, he wondered to himself.

As he walked down the narrow path between trees, the sun filtering through bare branches and casting long shadows, his thoughts once again drifted to his central question from several months prior: Why do we love?

Love brings trouble, the boy thought, his pace increasing with his angst. It feels wonderful at first, when it is still free, but when it becomes bound by commitment, promises and expectation, it dies a slow and gruesome death. Or maybe I just don't know how to do it. Or maybe what I feel for Mary isn't love.

Eventually he came to the stream and knelt hastily to drink from its crystal-clear waters. After drinking, Joseph stood just as quickly, his entire body still coursing with a certain tension, and as he did so, the blood drained from his head.

His world began to spin and he felt queasy. Then his vision went black, and within a few moments he crumpled, landing on the mossy bank next to the river, unconscious. Hitting the ground, he found himself amidst a vision.

He was seated before a fire. Around him, the desert in the depths of nocturnal dark bristled with life. In all directions came sounds of movement, of shifting sand, of breeze and of the flight of a hunting owl.

At once, Joseph noticed across the flames a man squatting low, adding a juniper branch to the already roaring blaze.

The man's suntanned skin was deeply creased from years of harsh exposure, and his hair was course, dark, braided, and adorned with barred, tawny and beige colored feathers.

As Joseph stared, the stranger rose to his feet and carried a small pouch over to someone laying at the perimeter of the firelight. Dipping two fingers into the pouch, he carefully applied a dark-colored paste to the abdomen of the man lying flat on his back upon the ground.

Joseph realized, after a long moment of disbelief, that the man lying on the ground was, in fact, himself. Perplexed, he arose and walked over to examine the body. It breathed, though in short, labored breaths. He could see mangled ribs on one side of the chest, and blood had dried across the face. The eyes were badly bruised and swollen, the jaw appeared askew, and a cut ran across the lower lip.

Joseph reached up to his own jaw and found it crooked in the same shape. Moving his fingers across his lips, he discovered a matching scar.

"How is this possible?" he wondered aloud. His voice startled him.

The man, without looking away from the task at which he worked, answered, "Something is troubling you."

"Well, I'm looking at my own body lying on the precipice of death in the desert. Wouldn't you be shaken by such an experience?"

The man smiled subtly. "Not really. But I've been around for a long time."

Joseph could look at his battered body no longer and returned to the fire.

After a time, the man returned to the fire as well and sat across from the boy. "Something is troubling you," he said again, and this time he stared straight into Joseph's eyes.

"You're right, but I don't know what it is."

The man stared intently but said nothing. The fire crackled between them and a breeze blew gently across Joseph's neck. After a time of searching the depths of the fire, Joseph spoke again, slowly, almost as though he were allowing a force greater than himself to loosen the cords which bound his heart.

"I have the love of a good woman. But I am enchanted by another. And still, I'm not sure why I should love at all."

Silence fell once more, the crackle of juniper singing in harmony with the crickets and soft wind.

The man spoke, "There is no path when you don't know what you want. So, choose."

The two sat in the quiet between them for a long time. Neither spoke. There was nothing to say. Joseph found that even his mind had been quieted by the gravity of the desert. The perfumed smoke from the fire before him rose in a crooked, winding column into the starry sky. A crescent moon caught the thread and it shone silver.

He considered the path that had led him to this place in life. He saw how it was crooked like the smoke but wound always somehow in the same upward direction. He saw, too, how even though the smoke always moved up, its destination was obscured by the darkness and stunning enormity of the endless sky. For a moment he wondered where his own life was headed. And as he thought about where his life might be going, he began to wonder again about what seemed to be a recurring question in his life at present: Why do we love?

A cautious stillness settled in the boy's soul and his heart began to conjure images of good loves it had known. Joseph saw before his eyes images of morning sun bathing Mary's hair in golden light as it filtered through the rippled glass of an old barn window. He recalled with affection how much he had wished God would freeze time, if only for a moment.

He remembered glances shared with pretty girls in the store or the marketplace or the square and how such simple exchanges had made his heart jump with delight and excitement.

He thought about watching Anna's hands as she showed him something in the workshop and how much he had grown to admire her. And he thought about the way that Elizabeth looked at Sam whenever he came home for the noon meal.

In his meandering thoughts, story after story poured forth – memory after memory – painting the boy's life in brilliant hues of passion and enjoyment. His heart throbbed as it recounted the gentle electricity of Mary's fingers through his hair, or the sweet, shy smile given him by Madeline, the owner of the white house with the red door.

But then his heart grew heavy and spoke with a sweet sorrow of the pain it had known. The familiar ache of missing Ellie returned, and Joseph clutched at his chest. His heart told, too, of the way it had been hurt by his father's drinking and all the bad that brought, even though all it had wanted was to be loved. And he thought of how even though he'd never felt it in return, he still loved his father.

"I suppose we love because we can't help it," Joseph said.

The man across the fire smiled knowingly. Joseph wondered half aloud how it could be that love could bring such delight and such sorrow. But a quiet voice inside him seemed intent that perhaps sorrow was not worse than joy, pain no worse than pleasure. That perhaps they were but two sides of the same feeling and that both bring depth to the experience of living. That both point the way to who a person is supposed to become.

He thought with fondness of the struggle he had encountered in the desert, the stranger's blows that had knocked him from consciousness but also freed him from his self-destructive behavior.

He considered how the depths of his sorrow in his old life had driven his motivation for change following his attack. He began to realize how his greatest achievements were driven as much by his failures as they were by his successes.

Suddenly, his pain seemed purposeful rather than pointless. Joseph smiled at the thought that perhaps his hardships were as fruitful as his pleasures. He began to wonder if perhaps his hardships were more fruitful. Soon his thoughts ran out and he was silent.

Joseph waited a long time, hoping that further insights might arise, but none came. His eyes refocusing, he saw the man across the fire staring at him with a broad smile on his face.

"Many choose to live life in the middle," he said. "Many seek a life of ease, rather than a life of challenge. They run from hard struggle, but avoid the greatest pleasures, too. In this way they resist love because they know that love brings pain as much as it brings pleasure.

"Some retreat into the hills where they believe life and its sorrows can no longer reach them. Others retreat into themselves, becoming closed off to the entire world. And usually, they believe they are happy because they are not sad. But in fact, they are dead because they are no longer living.

"Just because one experience brings joy and another brings sorrow, does not mean that either is good or bad. They are equal, and both carry a lesson."

Joseph said, half in response to the man, half as a realization of his own, "So, we love because loving brings depth to life. Whether it brings us joy, or challenges our very core, love brings a richness that makes life worth living."

The man smiled again. "And because we can't help it. It is our nature to love."

"But why am I so unhappy? I have love in many different forms and from many different people, and still there's this angst welling up inside me that I can't seem to figure out."

The man looked compassionately at Joseph. "Happiness is not the point. We all think it is. But the point is to find that which delivers purpose. That is the most important thing."

Joseph recalled his first memories of waking in the desert. He thought of how he'd been astonished to find his body in one piece, astonished, too, to be thinking lucid, concrete thoughts. He'd emerged from the grasp of death and he had chosen to live, perhaps for the first time in his entire life.

He could never have known the depths of the turmoil he would encounter in his new life without vices, nor the hardship that might come from the comforts of a town and a job and a home. To have all his needs met and still find himself in anguish over the complicated details of life, such as love and purpose... how unfair it all was!

Why couldn't he just be happy? What more could he want? And yet he did want more. There was something within him – some piece of him that was teased by a peculiar house within a normal town – that knew his life held greater treasures yet; that he was not ready to settle where he was.

He looked again at the man across the fire and remembered what he'd said; there's no path for someone who doesn't know what he wants. Joseph realized that, though he was well-tended-to, he had no idea what he actually wanted.

Everything he had he'd come by easily, often without even a second thought. He realized he hadn't chosen any of this. He had chosen only to say yes to opportunities – surely there was nothing wrong with that. But it hadn't been sought in accordance with a higher purpose, and as a result, all that now seemed to bring Joseph comfort, actually just made him feel trapped.

He didn't know what he wanted, and he didn't know where to go next. Except, Joseph realized, maybe he did know what he wanted. He wanted life. He wanted to live. Even if he didn't know exactly what that might look like, he knew that this current life wasn't bringing him the fulfilment he desired. Maybe it was enough, at least for now, to know what he didn't want... Maybe the answers would come.

In the dream, Joseph closed his eyes and inhaled deeply. The sounds of the desert began to change, and he began to hear the babbling of a swollen brook.

Overhead, the sun was hot against his face. His back was wet from lying on the moss and beads of sweat dripped from his forehead. Wearily, Joseph sat up taking stock of his surroundings. He must have passed out after taking his drink from the spring. How fortunate to have landed on soft ground, he thought to himself.

He recounted the vision from which he had just emerged. Who was that man he continued to see? Was he a manifestation of the spirit of the desert itself? Was he some strange, wise nomad who wandered the dreamland of sand and stone, telling the secrets of the world? Was he simply a dream?

Joseph's wondering was cut short by a dark shape emerging from the trees on the opposite bank of the creek. Though startled at first, he quickly realized it was the same dog that had roused him from his slumber that first afternoon in town. It drank briefly and then sat on its haunches, staring at the boy.

"What do you think?" he asked of the animal. "You probably think I'm crazy."

The dog broke into a pant and seemed to smile at him. Joseph leaned over and washed his face in the cold water.

Though his head swam with new thoughts, ideas and challenges, he felt less agitated and clearer than he had in months.

"Well what should we do now?"

The dog just continued to stare at him and pant, its tongue hanging from its mouth. He remembered the words of the man with the black braids and the feathers in his hair. *Choose* he had said.

"I suppose you're waiting for me to decide." Joseph chuckled. "It's terribly nice here. I think we should stay for a while. But not too long. I think the time is soon that we'll need to go on an adventure."

The dog lay down and rested its head on its paws. Joseph, too, lay back on the mossy bank and stared up at the canopy of trees. Fresh buds had begun to emerge and birds flitted about in all directions, gathering things with which to build their nests.

We love because to love is to be alive, he thought to himself. And I still have many adventures before me. It was a good feeling to finally be making sense of things again.

As the weeks wore on following Joseph's vision in the forest, his newfound clarity gave way to the same frustrated confusion that had permeated his soul in the months before.

Though he had known in that moment, lying on the bank, that new adventures awaited, he struggled to know how to seek them. He also found himself fearful of damaging the relationships he'd forged since arriving in the town the previous August, especially his relationship with Anna and Gabriel.

His relationship with Mary, though punctuated with sweetness, remained distant and tense. She wanted more of him while he sought space and autonomy. How he wished she could be satisfied with what he was able to give of himself. He didn't want to be rid of her, he just wanted a little more space, a little more time, and a little more freedom.

He also found himself seeking the company of Madeline more and more, often lingering for nearly an hour out front of her house, asking her all manner of questions about the plants in her garden, about her past, about anything he could imagine.

She remained friendly but detached, which tortured him, and often left him both giddy with admiration and furious at his apparent inability to woo her into a more intimate relationship.

Madeline was a wise woman. She seemed to know everything there was to know about the seasons, about soil conditions, about water. Her character was perpetually poised, giving nothing away, and yet leaving just enough room in Joseph's imagination that he continued to believe that one day he might win her favor. He had begun to believe that perhaps she was his next adventure.

Gabriel continued to grow increasingly concerned for his friend, but any effort he made to console him only pushed Joseph further away.

One night Gabriel broached the topic over dinner in the presence of Sister Anna. Joseph had been in a particularly foul mood. Upon his friend's questioning, he exploded in a resentful spew of frustrations at his life, at feeling trapped, and at feeling like he could no longer remember why he'd chosen to stay in this town. After standing abruptly and knocking his chair to the ground, he left in a storm of anger.

Sister Anna was speechless; Gabriel felt he had pushed too hard and worried that he may have ruined their relationship. But the woman assured him no permanent damage had been done and that Joseph would return in a few days' time. When he did, they could begin the process of healing the rift that had just formed. Still, Gabriel harbored regret and resentment, and scarcely slept for three days and nights until, finally, Joseph returned.

When he walked through the door of the humble cottage, his clothes were covered in sand, his hair was filthy, and his skin was darkened from days in the sun. Embarrassed by his actions and full of regret for having acted so selfishly to those who had cared so selflessly for him, Joseph kept his eyes low. Sister Anna checked him over and asked him to come in, sit down and have something to eat. He accepted.

Gabriel was out working in the barn and hadn't seen the older boy return. Anna took the opportunity to speak with Joseph privately.

"I remember the months before I decided to become a nun. I was miserable. I was doing the things I had always been told to do, but still life was bringing me no joy. It felt like every step I took was uphill. I could make no progress; I had no momentum.

"And then, one night I had a dream in which an angel appeared to me. He told me many things that night, but the one I remember most of all is this. He told me that if one's life is not bringing fulfilment, it is usually a sign that something must be changed. And when it feels like we can't go on any longer – like we've lost our way completely – our answers are soon revealed. He told me to be patient and remain open to divine guidance. 'It's always darkest before the dawn' he had said."

Joseph listened intently until Sister Anna was finished speaking, and after a moment of reflection decided to tell her about the vision he'd had by the river. He related how he had felt such peace and clarity after that vision, but that it had faded as he returned to the parts of his life that were causing particular anguish.

"The morning I woke up from my dream with the angel," Sister Anna responded, "I was more confused than ever. In my soul was the flicker of hope that perhaps life didn't have to be so agonizingly difficult and boring. But what I should do next remained shrouded in mystery.

"The next night I had a dream that I awoke in a convent at the edge of a mountain range. The sun poured through the window, and I could hear one of the other sisters humming as she tended the little garden outside.

"I felt such peace in that place, and such certainty within my own soul. When I awoke in my own bed the following morning, I went immediately to tell my mother. I explained what I had dreamt. She smiled at me as she had when I was a young girl, placed her hands on my shoulders and kissed my forehead.

"Then she said to me, 'The signs are clear, my daughter. You must go, and I know to where. I hope that someday you will return to me and continue the path of my father and his father before him, but if your path leads you to a pious life for the rest of your days, then I will be happy for you because you followed your heart.'

"My eyes filled with tears at my mother's words. Her support had been so selfless, so unconditional. I hugged her longer and tighter than I had ever hugged her before, and the very next day we began the journey to the convent."

Joseph was pensive. He understood Sister Anna's tale, and appreciated her desire to help him, but her advice had brought him no closer to figuring out the challenges he faced in his own life.

Then he remembered what the man had told him. "There is no path when you don't know what you want." What do I truly want, he wondered?

"In my vision, the man told me I needed to figure out what I wanted. How am I supposed to answer that? I want life – I want to live. But I'm doing that here, seeking new experiences where I can, and getting nowhere. I don't know what to do."

"Why did you come here?" Sister Anna asked. "And why did you stay?"

He considered her questions. "I came here because I was ready to begin a new life. And I stayed because everything seemed to flow so easily for me. I met Mary and grew fond of her immediately. I met you, and Gabriel, and you offered me such care and generosity. Even my position at the store came about without effort and brought me happiness."

"Are these things bringing you happiness now?"

Joseph frowned. "No." He was ashamed to speak with any negativity of the hospitality and welcome Sister Anna and Gabriel had so heartily extended to him.

"Perhaps it is just that this chapter has come to a close - or is coming to one - and it's better not to dwell too much on why."

Joseph was baffled by her resolve. How could she dismiss him so easily? How could she have given him so much without any expectation of him in return? Didn't she want him to stay?

"You are just beginning to live again. It's like learning to walk, Joseph. It's okay if the first steps cause you to stumble. Perhaps going back to the drawing board is in order, so you can explore what steps might come next."

The boy searched her face for some sort of judgement or frustration but found none. Instead, she stared back at him with a tremendous tenderness and strength.

"I don't know how to start over again," he said after a time.

"Well, you were reborn in the desert. You told me so the first night we met. Perhaps it is in the desert you will find your answers?"

Joseph looked to the floor. Considering this possibility felt like failure, and he didn't like it.

"Sleep on it for a few days. You have been away, and now you're here. Whatever you decide to do, I'm sure you'll make the right decision. Go and get cleaned up and then go and see Gabriel. He's been worried sick about you, and he feels terrible for driving you away. Mary came by looking for you as well. I think you have some conversations ahead of you. It's best you deal with these things first. Your answers will come."

The boy nodded and rose to leave. As he was stepping out the door he paused. "Does everyone see visions, or angels?" he asked her, turning to watch her expression.

"Whether others also have the experiences that you and I seem to have is not so important. What is important is that these visions help provide clarity in your life – and in mine. It is up to us to choose what to do with the things we learn."

He nodded again and left, closing the door behind him.

As Joseph washed himself, the cold water dripping off his skin in a stream of sandy sediment, he felt heavy. On his shoulders he carried the burden of an intentional life. He turned Anna's words over and over in his head. He knew he needed to confront the aspects of his life that weren't making him happy. Maybe I could just leave tonight without saying a word, he thought. It would be easiest to run.

But he knew running away would only lead to more anguish for himself and for those he loved. This was his opportunity to choose life in all its difficulty. This was part of the adventure: saying goodbye. Because he knew that only once he had closed the door on the old, would he be able to open the door to the new.

This was an opportunity for him to choose the life he wanted, even if he wasn't sure what it would look like. He just wished that his choice didn't have to be between hurting people he loved and following his heart.

He found Gabriel a while later in the kitchen. He had finished his chores and had come in for something to eat. When Joseph entered the house, Sister Anna ducked out saying she had forgotten something in another room. Gabriel was surprised to see his friend. Joseph guessed that Sister Anna hadn't mentioned his return. For a moment neither said anything. After a time, Gabriel began to speak but the older boy cut him off.

"I'm sorry for the way I behaved. I'm sorry I was angry with you. I'm sorry I stormed out. I'm sorry I've been so absent and that I've avoided the conversation you continue to bring up. You're right – I am not myself, and I am not confronting my challenges. You have only been trying to help me – both of you have – and I've treated you poorly. I'm ashamed, and I'm sorry."

He hadn't intended to be so vulnerable – his words surprised him. But he was glad he had said it now that it was out.

Gabriel seemed surprised as well. When at last he spoke, his voice was meek and barely audible. "Where did you go? I've been so worried about you."

"I know. I know. And I'm sorry I left like that. I've been around... I was in the forest, and in the desert. I didn't know where else to go. I scarcely slept; I haven't eaten. I walked and walked and yelled at the sky. My anger consumed me. But I came face to face with the decisions I must make, and I realized that I am not happy.

"Why are you smiling?"

"Because I have known that you are not happy, and I'm so grateful that you can see that for yourself. Joseph, when I met you in the late summer you were so full of life, and so in touch with yourself. It was as though life itself pulsed in your veins. But lately you've been as though dead. There's been no spark, no passion. And I've tried to help you see it - for a while I thought I could make you see it - but it's been no use.

"Now, you stand before me a different man. Your anger when you left was surprising, but it also gave me hope that you hadn't become completely consumed by your struggle. In your rage was a stubbornness - a refusal to succumb to quiet desperation.

"And today I see that you are choosing your path once again."

"Gabriel, I've judged you harshly. You deserve much more credit than I've been willing to give. You are a wise young man, and I am grateful to call you a friend."

There was a pause as Gabriel smiled. "Have you seen Mary? She came by here looking for you. She seemed distressed to learn you hadn't been here either."

"No, I only got back a short while ago, and aside from you and Sister Anna I haven't spoken to anyone. To be honest, I am not prepared for the conversation I need to have with Mary."

Gabriel answered, "I think I know what you mean. Do you plan to end things with her?"

Joseph paused, deep in thought. Then he diverted his eyes. "Not exactly."

"What do you mean? Are you going to stay with her? Have you had a change of heart?" He seemed boyishly hopeful for a moment.

"No. I need to find my clarity. I need to go back to the desert, but this time I'm not coming back. Not here at least. This chapter is ending now."

Gabriel was quiet. The smile had disappeared from his face, and he appeared as though he were going to cry.

"So, what? Is this just the end for you then? Just like that? You're going to go off and die somewhere alone?"

"Gabriel, no! That's not it at all! In fact, all I want right now is to truly live. As you've said, I have not been living these last few months. I'm going into the desert to find my path in life once again, because I see now I've lost my way. And though I don't know how long I'll be away, or where I'll go next, I know for certain that I will not be coming out of the desert the same man I am today. And I won't be coming back here. But rest assured, I will come back out of the desert."

"I believe you. I have no choice but to believe you. Of course I'm sad, because you have been a good friend; the best friend I have known. But my sadness is mine to carry. So instead, I give you my blessing. I'd also like to give you this knife."

His eyes glistening, he produced a small knife from his front pocket. It had a folding blade and a handle made of bone, finely etched with a scene portraying a hunt on horseback.

Joseph recognized it at once as the one Gabriel had used to whittle by the riverside on the day of their meeting, though he hadn't noticed the intricate beauty of the handle.

"Gabriel, this knife is beautiful. There's no way I can accept it."

"You have to. I insist. This knife was my fathers – or that's what the sisters at the orphanage told me. It is one of only two things I have from my parents. The other is a locket that belonged to my mother. Joseph, you have been like a brother to me, and for that, I want you to hold a piece of my history. Keep it close, and may it keep you safe."

Joseph stared in astonishment at the gift and at the boy who held it out to him.

Carefully, solemnly, he extended his hand to accept it. Taking the knife in his own hand, he took his friend in a long, firm embrace. Gabriel had been like a brother to him as well, and this recognition of their bond almost made Joseph reconsider his determination to find his peace elsewhere. How could he leave behind the first real friend he'd ever had? How could he leave behind a brother? But he knew he had to go. He had tried everything in this town and continued nonetheless to feel increasingly anxious.

"I need to go find Mary," Joseph said at last.

"Good luck," Gabriel said earnestly. "Your heart is strong and so is hers. This may hurt, but it won't break you. Either of you."

Mary was working in the garden planting some seeds as Joseph approached from the direction of town. When she looked up and saw him coming she thought to herself that maybe he was coming to meet her parents, and that he had finally come to his senses. She jumped up and ran to him and met him a ways from the house, and her mother stood in the doorway watching, unable to hear their conversation.

Her excitement at seeing him had quickly faded into confusion, denial and eventually anguish as she came to understand the meaning of his visit. He hadn't come to join her more wholly - he had come to tell her goodbye.

He spoke clearly and directly, leaving no doubt as to his chosen path. She wept quietly, staring into his eyes, begging him to change his mind and stay. She couldn't understand why he had to leave, and she especially couldn't understand why he wouldn't come back.

Didn't he love her? Wasn't he happy with her? Hadn't she made him feel something real? Of course, she had, and he told her so. But he remained resolute in his decision, and after a short time, after holding her for a short time as she cried into his shoulder and held him like a life raft, he kissed her once and turned to walk back into town.

As he walked away, her tears still wet upon the shoulder of his shirt, he felt that strange sensation that comes when someone has done something gruesome and necessary. The grotesque mixture of relief and self-loathing and despondence weighed in his chest and made his footsteps heavy. He was relieved at having faced the difficult conversation head-on and having come out the other side. But inside, his heart was still breaking. He broke for Mary; for that kind, innocent girl who had loved him with everything she had. He broke for the possibilities he had once imagined with her, and for the future they would never have. He broke because he had just realized how much he had loved her, and how much he was going to miss her demands of him. Even her impossible nature and neediness had taken on a certain nostalgic sweetness.

We only appreciate what we've had once it's gone, he thought to himself. It had happened with Gabriel, and now with Mary. As the door closed on each of those relationships, he had seen them in their waning glory for much more than he had perceived to that point.

Perhaps that's how it is, he thought. He wondered how he might harness the appreciation before the final closing; how he might recognize the gifts he'd been given before they were gone.

These thoughts spun circles in his head as he walked through town and he hardly noticed where he was going. In time he found himself near to Sam and Elizabeth's house. After a moment of consideration, he decided to stop by to bid Sam farewell, and to thank him and Elizabeth both for their hospitality and support.

Sam shook his hand and bade him goodbye. Elizabeth gave him a warm, lingering hug with well wishes in her eyes and sweet smile on her face. She sent him along with a kitchen rag full of biscuits. Joseph thanked them both one last time and turned to leave.

It was nearly dark before he turned onto the lane at the end of which sat Anna and Gabriel's house. As he drew close, the dog came trotting out of the woods and walked beside him.

"What, now I need to say goodbye to you too?" he asked the animal.

It just continued to trot along next to him.

"Oh, you think you're coming with me, do you?"

Maybe it would be good to have a companion, he thought.

When he at last entered the home of Sister Anna that evening, he found the table set for a feast. While he'd been out, she had butchered two chickens, and the table was piled high with all manner of foods.

"Gabriel told me. If you will be leaving tomorrow, I thought we had better celebrate tonight." She smiled as she spoke, seeing the surprise on Joseph's face.

"I didn't say I was leaving tomorrow... how did you know?" Joseph asked, glancing from Sister Anna to Gabriel and back again.

Sister Anna and Gabriel caught each other's gaze. Then she spoke. "You have made up your mind to go, and you have already said your goodbyes. We all know that you will be gone with first light. When a man has made up his mind, every moment spent in delay brings him another inch closer to death. If he waits too long, he loses all resolve and the choice is no longer his.

"Now let's eat. Tonight is about celebrating. It's about celebrating a good man and time spent in good company. It's about celebrating following the path of one's heart. And it's about the honest fight to live a life full of greatness and adventure."

She raised her glass and Joseph toasted with his own as tears pressed against the corners of his eyes. Hers was a good, pure love, and he was grateful for having been able to experience it. It was the first time he'd felt love without the burden of obligation. It freed something inside him.

After the feast, Joseph and Gabriel went out to walk amongst the foothills under a full moon. They talked as though their friendship wasn't in its final moments and laughed at jokes only boys would find funny.

By the time he finally crawled into bed, Joseph was exhausted and in no time at all, he had fallen asleep.

He awoke before dawn. The previous night, he'd laid out the few things he chose to bring. Sister Anna had given him a small ruck he could carry on his shoulders, and in it he had packed some food to last a few days, a canteen, a jacket he'd bought from Sam's store over the winter, a flint for starting fires, and a bottlecap he'd found in his pocket when he first awoke in the desert. The last item he treasured perhaps most of all because it reminded him of the life he had once lived. And it gave him reason to keep moving forward.

On the stool by his bed sat the knife Gabriel had given him. He had almost placed it in his bag but decided at the last moment to store it tucked in his belt instead. He wasn't sure why, but a small voice told him it would come in handy. He felt a sense of pride sliding it between his pants and his belt, as though he were a proper man, setting out on a great adventure. He had known a good friend and he carried a piece of his memory at his hip.

This is how it is, he thought. Here I go, setting out on another adventure, wearing clothes from a woman I've loved, with a knife from a brother shoved in my belt, and having been fed and sheltered on my last night by the purest of hearts. I suppose we can't help but to take pieces of our past on our journeys into the unknown.

He realized he felt the imprints of all these people upon his heart as much as he felt their articles upon and all around his body.

Fully dressed and feeling both excited and solemn, he rose, splashed some water on his face from the bucket by the door, took a swig from the ladle, and swung the ruck over his shoulder.

Before leaving, he made the bed and placed a bundle of money on the pillow with a note, thanking Sister Anna for all she'd given him. He knew she would resent him for payment left against her will, but it felt right to repay her generosity.

The sun was just beginning to illuminate the horizon when he opened the front door. Joseph was reminded of the morning he had left the desert, and how the sun had greeted him as he walked, just as it would this day.

Something stirred at his feet. Looking down, his eyes adjusting to the meager dawn, he realized the dog had spent the night sleeping on the threshold. Had it been waiting for him? A part of him doubted the dog would follow for long. Still, he felt a glimmer of hope at the idea of a traveling companion. Thinking to win the animal's favor, he threw it a small corner of a biscuit. The dog ate it in a single bite and looked to Joseph for more.

Breathing deep the cool morning air, he felt intensely alive. He looked up the road, then the other way. In one direction lay the town he had called home for nearly a year. In the opposite direction lay his future, unknown and inhospitable as it may be. Joseph closed his eyes, feeling especially fulfilled, and realized how long it had been since he'd felt this way.

Sister Anna is a wise woman, he thought to himself. She knew what I needed even before I did. I hope that someday I will be able to help another, the same way she has helped me.

For a moment he wondered how long he would have stayed trapped in the same, monotonous cycle, had she not sat him down. But he caught himself and decided that he would no longer allow his past to define his future. He would learn from his mistakes, certainly, but no good could come from worrying about what might have been,

The first rays of sun crested the foothills to the east and Joseph felt an overflowing gratitude at the immensity of the great beyond. His heart leapt, eager to join with it.

He took one step. Then another. Then another. Before he knew it, he was at the end of the lane and Anna's cottage had vanished from sight.

"Well, I guess there's no looking back now," he said to the dog, still trotting at his side.

It just continued to walk, and Joseph did the same. As he stepped in time to a song he sung in his head, he thought with a smile, here I go; off to find the rest of my life.

Part 3

Day 1

Joseph and the dog walked all morning without pause. Well-rested and energized by the excitement of adventure, they made good progress, and by the time the sun was high in the sky, the foothills were a distant mirage amidst an otherwise vast desert.

The boy marveled at how different this landscape looked compared to the one that had delivered him into the town the previous August. Where that had seemed an endless expanse of nothing but dried-up earth and quiet, meek flora clinging to life through acts of sheer persistence, the scene before him was breathtaking.

In all directions he could see explosions of color. Flowering plants shone vivid hues of pink and gold, even their stems enlivened with velvety green and shades of purple.

Above him the sky seemed a starker blue than in the autumn, and the sand a redder, move vibrant shade. Everywhere the contrasts of plant and stone, each thing in its own place and not crowding in upon each other. The desert must be immensely proud of its beauty, he thought.

The animals, too, seemed to be more active. Tracks crisscrossed his path, lizards darted from one bush to the shade of another right under his feet, and he sensed himself to be the subject of fascination for a few crows that continued to play their thrill-seeking games above him.

It seemed that each breath Joseph drew was deeper than the last. He held his head high as he walked, and took his time with each step, making sure it fell in line with the rhythm of his heart and his breathing.

For the first time in many months, he felt a synchronicity between his body and the earth, as though they were once again speaking the same language. Thinking this, he stopped to remove his shoes. As he knelt the dog came up to sit beside him, and he noticed – or perhaps sensed – that the animal was thirsty. Sinking one foot and then the other into the warming sand, he felt the course softness filter between his toes.

Looking up, he noted the position of the sun and thought it wise to seek water and stop for a rest. He wasn't tired, but he knew the dangers of heat and dehydration. Standing, now barefoot, he surveyed his surroundings. A ways to the west he noticed what appeared to be a corridor of green snaking through an otherwise red horizon. He signaled towards it and the dog didn't disapprove. The sand was hot underfoot, but not unbearably so. He put his shoes in his bag and continued on.

Upon reaching the creek he was met by yet another miracle of the desert which he had not expected.

Having crossed its sands in the late, dry summer months, he had been hard pressed to find water flowing above ground. He knew he had been incredibly fortunate to have found that pool.

But now that winter had passed and spring was upon him, water was abundant, clear and cool. This water probably began its journey in the hills from which we ourselves have come, he thought as he bent to fill a canteen. He considered how many traveling companions he had come by already on this short journey. Whether his dog, or the water, or the crows overhead, he felt in good company.

The dog drank heartily from the stream and lay down in a shady spot to rest. Joseph was more curious than weary. Climbing a cottonwood along the riverbank he rose above the desert floor in pursuit of a higher vantage point. He wasn't sure how long he'd be staying in the desert, nor where he would go next. A piece of him – a more cautious, less wild piece – was already feeling satisfied with his walk and was quietly hoping he might spy another settlement.

He had reached the part of every journey where the adventurer questions his own motives and begins for a moment to long for the comforts of home. The enormity of his solitude and its contrast to the companionship of his last several months had stirred a certain anxiety. But he quieted his worry and scanned the horizon. Seeing nothing but sand, stone and water, he sat back on a branch to rest, allowing the slight breeze to cool him.

In the heat, he began to doze, but was awakened a short time later by the barking of the dog. Looking down, he saw a coyote slowly approaching their spot by the river.

Joseph was frozen. Surely this animal couldn't be trying to harm his companion, but why else would it be approaching this particular spot on the river when plenty of others were available?

Suddenly, the coyote lunged forward, the dog jumped back, and Joseph realized why it had come. Before he could get to the ground, the coyote had grabbed his bag, along with all his food, his jacket and his flint. In a flash, it was gone, sprinting through the sagebrush with its spoils in tow.

The dog took off after it and Joseph followed, hollering with all his might. After a wicked chase, the animal had gained enough ground that the boy realized he had lost the race. The dog wasn't losing any ground, but it wasn't gaining either. Joseph whistled and it stopped, looking back at him, incredulous that he would allow such a transgression without a fight.

Joseph sat down in the sand, panting. His chest heaved, his brow dripping with sweat. After a time he caught his breath. He needed water now more than ever. He looked back and realized how far he'd run. A half-mile to the west he could see the river.

He began to retrace his steps and was joined by the dog as he walked. A few hundred feet from the river, something bright red caught his eye at the base of a juniper bush. Reaching down, he realized it was his bottle cap. It must have fallen out, he thought, and he picked it up, putting it in his pocket. As he did so, he remembered Gabriel's knife stuck in his belt. He was glad he'd kept that with him instead of putting it in the bag.

I should listen to my intuition more often, he thought to himself.

Eventually, he arrived back at the river. After a long drink, and after washing his sweaty face in the running water, he lay back in the sand, staring up at the trees and the striking blue of the sky beyond.

"You probably think this is some kind of joke, eh?" he said aloud to no one in particular.

The animal had taken all their food, and now they would have to find their own sustenance. He'd known they would eventually need to hunt or scavenge, but he had not planned to begin that task so soon. And though he wouldn't have admitted it outwardly, Elizabeth's biscuits and a few provisions from Sister Anna had been a comforting tether to the life he'd known. With them gone, he suddenly felt exposed and very alone. The heat, the water, and the adrenaline washed him in weariness, and he again fell into a slumber.

As he slept, he dreamed.

Nine blackbirds flew above him in broad circles. Three were very loud, their shrill calls shattering the serenity of the mid-day heat. Three others made the occasional call, but were not so brash as the first. And the last three remained silent.

The birds flew this way and that, each with its own pattern of calling.

Then, from the corner of his mind's eye he saw a raptor with tail feathers of bright red emerge and cross the sky directly above him. At once the crows took to intimidating the intruder. They dove at the hawk, the loudest ones calling incessantly as they did so.

But the redtail remained steadfast in its path of flight and seemed not the least bit bothered by the crow's harassing games.

A few times, a crow came so close to the hawk's wings that it lost balance and had to correct. But it continued forever towards its destination: a massive juniper, gnarled limbs reaching skyward.

Finally it landed atop the highest mangled branch and perched with regal gravity. It seemed to dare the crows to challenge it there. But they didn't. Instead they took back to the skies and went about their business of circling and cawing. Joseph stayed fixated on the hawk for a long while, watching its stillness, awed and transfixed by its power.

How can something convey such strength and determination simply by sitting - simply by existing - he thought to himself.

Then, in a startling break from its stoicism, the hawk leapt off the branch and dove towards the sand, landing in an audible collision which threw clouds of dust in all directions.

After a brief struggle, a blur of feathers and sage, the hawk emerged, carrying a snake dangling from its talons. Again it landed on its juniper perch and began to devour its prey, which still wriggled in its grasp.

Joseph roused slowly. The sun had shifted such that it now shone directly on his feet, and they were burning. Sitting up, he noticed the dog asleep in the shade at the base of a tree. As he moved, the dog picked its head up, ears perked in inquisitive attention. His stomach grumbled and he cursed the coyote for stealing his food.

He moved slowly, still heavy from sleep. As he did the dog came to the base of the tree, tail wagging.

"What are you so happy about?" he asked the animal.

It leapt up and out of the shallow bank of the river and waited for him to follow.

"Then I guess we should move onward. What do you think about following the river for a while?"

The dog just stared at him, panting.

I probably have a week or so before I really get into trouble from hunger, he thought to himself. With water and warmth and the safety of the cottonwood corridor, he realized he actually had very little to worry about. Breathing deeply, he allowed himself to ease back into the thrill of the adventure. The wave of uncertainty had passed, and he was again grateful for the journey that lay before him.

It was nearly dark when they stopped walking. Boy and dog drank side by side from the creek and then leaned back against a tree to rest.

I suppose I'll have to figure out how to make fire without my flint, he thought. He recalled a conversation with Sam.

The man had told him about some of the ways to make fire without modern tools. Joseph had been fascinated.

For a time, Sam had befriended an old trapper named Icarus who occasionally came through town to trade furs and buy tools and liquor. Through their conversations, he'd learned – at least in theory if not in practice - all manner of survival skills, which Sam had likewise found fascinating. Everything from improvising shelter to building snares to trap game. Of course, his demonstration of the skills was limited to the various items around the shop, but Joseph had learned a great deal, nonetheless.

As he thought on the various methods Sam had talked about, he remembered being struck by the simplicity of a certain method called a hand drill. The premise was that a straight rod, carved to a dull point on one end, was placed inside a divot carved into a flat piece of wood. The flat piece would rest on the ground, the rod would be held between the palms, and the point rested inside the divot.

Then, using both hands, palms open and holding the rod between them, one would rub their hands together such that the rod twisted in place. The friction and resulting heat would eventually generate a small spark, which could be used to catch light to a bit of hair or juniper husk or other suitable fire starter.

Joseph surveyed his surroundings. The riverbank was littered with sticks. Sam had mentioned that cottonwood and yucca were both ideal woods to use for hand drills.

Joseph smiled to himself. But as he thought to rise to gather wood and fashion his tools, he let out a yawn. "You know what, old friend, I think we should sleep tonight. We can always have our campfire tomorrow."

The dog didn't stir. It was also tired from the heat and the walk and had fallen asleep promptly upon arriving. Joseph, too, felt a wave of fatigue wash over him. He lay back and folded his forearms beneath his head. The sky above was endless and star filled. Even with the waning full moon, the heavens rolled out in all directions like a cosmic blanket, soft and comforting. The stars above seemed so close to the boy that he could reach up and touch them.

Around him, crickets rose up in song. Beside him the creek gurgled past, lapping at stones and silt in its path. And beneath him, the sand and stone retained the day's warmth, filling him with a simple satisfaction.

In the depths of his soul, not a thought stirred. He smiled at the realization that just 48 hours before he had felt so conflicted, so torn, so at war with himself. And yet, here he was on this night, tired, sore and dirty, but filled to the brim with a hunger for life itself, and experiencing fully every single second of it.

In the early morning hours, in the time before sunrise when the sky takes on a cerulean glow and the desert exists in a space between the worlds of life and death, Joseph again began to dream.

He had just jumped down as the coyote had snatched his bag and taken off across the sand. He ran furiously, sprinting with all his might. The dog was hot in pursuit as well.

The coyote seemed to be running straight for a cliff, and he felt a victorious fire rise up from within him. He'd won. But as the coyote reached the edge of the cliff, the bag in its jaws, it jumped.

Before Joseph's eyes the animal transformed into a large hawk with flaming tailfeathers of amber, still clutching the bag in its talons. It soared effortlessly across the canyon as the boy looked on in disbelief. On the other side he caught sight of a man standing alone, also watching the bird.

Though he was far away on the distant side of a canyon cliff, the boy recognized him as the man from his previous visions. The blanket he wore over his shoulders blew slightly in the breeze and he watched the bird as it flew towards him.

As it passed overhead, it dropped the bag and the man caught it. Closing his eyes, he inhaled a deep breath and smiled towards the sky. And as he held the bag up towards the heavens, the bag itself vanished into a blinding white light.

Day 2

He noticed the hunger first.

But it was not the angry hunger of malnourishment. It was simply an emptiness, a void. Within his stomach he felt the familiar feeling of longing he'd felt in his heart during his later months in the town. In his grogginess he thought it interesting that both the heart and the stomach can experience hunger.

As he began to come more fully awake, he remembered the dream in vivid flashes of recollection. He understood - or chose to accept a belief - that the coyote had been merely acting out the will of the desert. Joseph recalled the communion he had felt with the sand and the sun the previous day, and he thought it all made a bit more sense. Somehow it all fit perfectly together, even if he couldn't understand the big picture.

Maybe I don't need to understand the path I'm on, he thought, but that doesn't mean I can't follow it.

"Are you hungry?" he asked the dog. But it hardly stirred from its slumber. He thought it strange and comforting that this animal had chosen to accompany him on his journey. For a moment he wondered if the animal even knew what it had gotten itself into. Well, he thought, the dog's free to go anytime it decides. No sense worrying about it.

The first light of morning was growing in the sky and the coldest period of day was upon them. In the desert, it is always coldest just after the sun comes up, when the earth has finally released all its last reserves of heat, but before the sun has had a chance to warm it again. The chill air felt good in his lungs, but it drove him to enough discomfort that he decided to try his hand at making a fire.

Gathering his sticks and pulling the knife from his belt, he began to sharpen and divot. Before long, he had fashioned his implements and gathered kindling.

He set to work with the hand drill. He had little success at first, but once he found his rhythm he found it easy to get the wood to warm and eventually spark. The work took a heavy toll on his tender hands, but his sheer determination overtook the pain, and he persisted until he succeeded in coaxing a spark from his implements.

Still, it was mid-morning by the time his fire was going, and he found it too hot with the sun now overhead, so he put it out.

The two wanderers decided to stay put for the day and to spend that night next to the river. Joseph hoped the coals would keep warm under the sand where he had buried them, and that he could easily start up the fire that evening. Besides, he had nowhere to be, so he thought it wise to take the day to relax and explore.

Though an emptiness had settled into his middle, he didn't feel particularly hungry, and certainly not enough to go seek out food.

This is all part of the Desert's plan, he thought.

But when a person stops thinking about their next meal, they often find that they have an abundance of time on their hands. People spend a lot of time eating, and thinking about eating, he thought to himself.

In order to decide what to do next, Joseph thought he'd get a good look around. He knew he'd be able to find their camp no matter how far he strayed, because the river was visible for miles in all directions, and at least he could follow it until he reached their spot.

He chuckled as he considered his concept of *their* camp, which was marked only by some coals glowing under the sand. How easily we attach to our places, he thought as he climbed the sloping trunk of a cottonwood to get a better view. His eyes came to rest upon a large juniper growing seemingly out of nowhere some thousand feet to the southeast. Around it grew modest sage and rabbitbrush, but this tree was the king of its keep.

It rose in an ancient dance, its limbs elaborately formed and wild as the wind itself. Some sections had died off, but their wooden architecture stood strong against sandstorms and blazing heat, flowing like bones and muscle, inanimate and unyielding.

I want to go there, he thought, and climbed down from his perch.

The heat was fierce, the wind all but absent. He was grateful for the shade by the time he reached his destination.

He sat a while, his back against the tree, and watched the dog chase rabbits from bushes.

"You'll never catch one, boy. They're too quick for you." But he wondered if perhaps the dog could catch one. He might prove to be a more helpful traveling companion than the boy initially thought.

He watched the rabbits, too. He observed how they froze, then bolted. It was as though they didn't believe fully in their camouflage, and felt it necessary to burst from their safe cover to avoid capture.

But more often than not, he didn't even see them until they ran for safety. He wondered if the dog was able to see them in their frozen state. He also wondered if the hawks and owls and coyotes could sniff them out even though their positions appeared safe from his perspective.

There must be a reason they run, he thought, or perhaps we all just doubt ourselves and end up getting into trouble because of it. Our fear betrays us.

He noticed that their patterns of movement were different depending on whether or not they were being pursued. When wary of observation, but without a chase, the rabbits would dart from one shady bush to another before freezing once more.

If a chase ensued, the prey would weave back and forth through bushes and sandy banks, achieving incredible speed, and eventually disappearing down a hole at the base of one shrub or another. It was then he began to wonder if perhaps it was all a game to the rabbits.

People take plenty of dangerous risks in the name of fun, he thought. Crows certainly do it. Why not rabbits?

Maybe it's the thrill of the chase that gives them reason for living.

He thought back to his former life – the life blurred by alcohol and aimlessness – and how, even though he was severely impaired for many of those years he had also had his thrills. And most of those thrills had come on the precipice of death. Whether in the bar fights, or jumping the trains, or running off wild horses.

His thoughts drifted to his time in the town, and he realized that, in the name of responsibility and resolve, he had abandoned his reckless ways altogether. Perhaps that was what had led him to feel so bland and trapped. He'd swung too far toward the stoic and it had come back to bite him.

He felt certain there must be a middle way – a compromise. No; compromise implied sacrifice. And he was seeking both the fullness of stability and the enrapturing rush of a life lived at the edge. He wondered if both were possible.

The edge. In a flash of memory he recalled the night spent by the pool in the desert the year before, nearly dead from hunger and dehydration. He had lunged maniacally towards a cricket and nearly fallen off the ledge of a steep canyon wall. He had caught himself at the last moment. And in that moment, when he had danced with death and watched it float away without taking his hand, he had felt more alive, more vividly awake and aware, than he could ever remember.

Or when he awoke in the desert the very first time, not dead from the assault but close to it, and somehow feeling vividly alive anyway. Hanging on the edge of death, teetering there. Nearly falling off but pulling himself back together again.

See, I don't need alcohol to kill me, he thought, I do a damn good job of it myself most of the time. He chuckled.

In that moment he was pleased to be sitting in the desert, once again facing hunger and isolation, and once again feeling strikingly alive. "Hello, old friend," he said to the desert, smiling.

He was roused from his contemplation by a flash of black as the dog darted past him in hot pursuit of another catch. The beast exploded from the bushes, more focused and ravenous than he'd ever seen it. It clawed at the ground as puffs of sand and sage flew skyward, its only objective to catch its prey.

The rabbit wove in and out of a minefield of cactus, jumped clear over low-growing patches of shrubs, and scratched audible marks against sandstone outcroppings. The dog followed every step with a skill and speed that stunned the boy.

In a final lunge, it seized its catch, snatching it from the air as it tried in a last, desperate attempt to lose its pursuer. The two – dog and rabbit; predator and prey – tumbled to the ground as one, merging into one being of black and tan. The dog never fumbled its prize, and the rabbit, after a shriek not unlike that of a child, went limp in the dog's jaws. But Joseph noticed it was still breathing. It was playing dead.

The dog seemed taken aback. With the rabbit held loosely in its jaws, it looked to the boy as if to ask what to do next.

"Well, that's up to you. I guess you can eat it if you want. Or play with it. You earned it."

But after a moment the dog put it down in the sand and sat back on its haunches to watch it. Eventually, when the rabbit didn't move, the dog lay down and rested its head on its front paws. It stared intently. So did the boy.

Finally the rabbit stirred, looked around warily, and ran for cover. And though the dog picked up its head, its ears pricked attentively forward, it didn't rise or give chase. It merely watched, as though satisfied that it had caught the rabbit in the first place.

"I guess we won't be having rabbit for dinner. Or breakfast."

The dog lay its head on its paws once more and looked at the boy in such a way that Joseph felt bad for his comment.

"It's alright. We've always got crickets."

It was dark by the time Joseph made his way back to the river. He'd spent all day sitting under the juniper, lazily watching the sun move across the desert landscape. A few times he had risen to walk out amongst the sand, to investigate something or other, or simply to move his legs. At other times his eyes had grown heavy and he'd nodded off to sleep, his mind filled with images of women and animals, scenes from his past, or memories of his youth.

In the late afternoon he set off to wander in the general direction of the river, hoping to catch its path further south from their camp and follow the emerald snake back north to the place where he looked forward to sitting at the fire long into the night.

All that day, he'd marveled with a tinge of selfish pride that he wasn't yet feeling any substantial hunger. Even when he was more active, walking under mid-day sun or chasing minnows in the shallows of the creek, he felt more enlivened than starved.

But by the time he reached his camp he found himself beginning to think about food. He pushed the thought from his mind. I don't need it, he said to himself. It's not time yet. To satiate his shrinking stomach, he drank long and deep from the crystal waters and reveled in the sweetness.

The dog had continued to play its rabbit games for much of the afternoon. A few times it had found the bones of long-dead animals amongst the sand. It grabbed them and trotted off in some seemingly purposeful direction, bone held high in its jaws like some hard-won prize. Eventually, it had stashed its treasures in shallow holes scattered across the arid plain.

Joseph chuckled at the sight of his companion looking so wild in the vast landscape of sand and sage, looking so alive and youthful. When he had set off in search of the river, the dog had not followed, and he hadn't tried to coax it along.

Maybe this is where we part ways, he thought. Surely the dog would do fine to survive out here; it had already proven itself a worthy hunter. If only it would learn to eat its catch.

It was dark, and Joseph had started up his buried fire once again. The crickets chirped and their song delivered such solace that his contentment felt like it might spill out of his chest. Still the dog had not returned, and when he thought of it, he felt a brief pang of sadness at the idea that perhaps he would be continuing on alone.

But these shards of soulful contemplation did nothing to deter his happiness.

Here I am, sitting next to a fire, the river flowing before me, the sky stretched out above me, and my body reveling in the still simplicity of rest.

The thoughts flowed like lyrics and seemed to join voices with the river itself.

Then he heard the hoot of an owl. He looked up towards the branches above and could just make out the silhouette of a large raptor with rounded head, perched towards the top of the cottonwood on the opposite bank.

Against the velvet sky it was majestic. It swiveled its head back and forth, scanning the earth and its bounty as the customers in the shop used to do when looking for something in particular.

In silence, the boy looked on. Then he heard another hoot, this time from further away. The bird above him froze, the delicate breeze ruffling its feathers ever so slightly.

Then it called back, its voice deep and rich as a baritone woodwind. It seemed almost solid, the sound it made. As though one could bounce a rock off it. His neck began to ache from looking upward, so he lay back in the sand and continued to watch.

The calling continued in otherworldly reverberations. The desert itself seemed to listen. Near his feet, the fire crackled and cast long, dancing shadows against the underbelly of the trees overhead, warding off the growing dark. The sky now a deep blueish purple, the bird a hooded figure barely visible amongst its leafy keep.

Then action. The bird lifted weightlessly from its position and swooped in silence towards the ground some hundred feet away. It was like a graceful fall, its body leaning off the branch, the invisible wind catching its wings and propelling it forward. Joseph sat upright and craned his head to follow its path.

As it cruised noiselessly a few feet above the brush, it suddenly dove, talons outstretched. A scene from a silent movie. It rose from the brief chaos with a hare in its grasp, powerful wings beating great gusts of nothingness against the sandy floor. The boy looked on in amazement, astonished at its raw power and envious of the ease with which it could subsist in such a foreboding landscape.

After the owl, there was nothing but the sounds of the elements dancing together in his awareness. Water lapped playful soliloquies at its sandy banks. The desert released its daytime heat to the heavens. The wind and the fire held a lively conversation in soft whispers of crackling juniper. All seemed harmonious, and eventually sleep took the boy from his body and delivered him to other worlds.

He dreamed he was soaring high above the earth, looking down upon a broad and endless sandscape. Here and there rocks broke the boundless desert, but the dunes and valleys dominated.

Nothing stirred, save the sand which blew from one heap to another in an endless, maniacal rearranging. No water, no life. Only sand and more sand, and where it ended along the horizon, a vast, blue sky.

After a time, he saw the beginnings of foothills. Sparse and unassuming at first, they quicky grew into a labyrinth of rocks and mountains.

There at the base, he saw the dog running, its ears pointed forward, its body muscular. It dominated the terrain, fording effortlessly ahead through a sea of sand and stone.

Further ahead, he saw a pack of wolves, different shades of white and grey, loping towards the dog. He tried to call out, eager to protect his companion, but he was unable to make a sound. The animals continued on their collision course.

The pack crested a ridge, the base of which the dog was just reaching. The leader stood at the top, staring down at the lone dog and held its head high, ears at attention, tail rigid and commanding. But the dog didn't stop. Didn't it see the wolves? Didn't it know they would kill it?

It continued to run, up, up towards the ridge where the pack waited. As it drew close, it slowed to a trot and picked its way up the rocks towards the peak.

And then, at once, it was on the same level as the pack. The dog approached, alert and intentional, seemingly unafraid. The wolves held their ground, the leader walking towards the newcomer with a directness that startled the boy.

He was certain that at any moment the pack would eviscerate his companion and there was nothing he could do about it. But they didn't fight. No beast snarled; no hackles raised. Instead, the dog walked proudly through the group, sniffing at the leader as it passed, and lay down in their midst. And when it did so, the others lay down as well while the leader sat proudly upon his perch and scanned the desert expanse below.

Joseph looked on in astonishment. Though his mind couldn't make sense of the scene, in his heart he knew that the dog had become one with the wilderness. He understood that his companion wouldn't be continuing along with him on his journey.

And though he felt a sadness, he also felt a longing to join with it. To merge with the wild within was like an eager flame inside of him, drawing him towards his own unbecoming, and it flared in his soul.

C

The cold woke him. But there was a warmth on his side, and he realized as he regained the use of his faculties that the dog had curled up beside him at some point in the night.

Smiling, Joseph lay back his head and rested his hand atop the dog's withers, thinking back to his constant wondering if he would be abandoned by his companion. He wondered how his intuition could have been so wrong, but also found himself questioning whether it was intuition that had been speaking, or if it might have been fear. Perhaps fear and intuition speak the same language, he thought.

Before long he had drifted back to sleep.

Day 3

J oseph awoke to the sun's first light pressing in on the night. It seemed as though the sun had seen it fit to rouse both the boy and the desert from their restful slumber long before they themselves were ready. A piece of him resented it.

But he was wide awake, without a shred of drowsiness, so he sat up and reached skyward in a stretch.

The dog, too, roused and looked about itself, seeming to take stock of its predicament. It landed its gaze upon the boy as it rose to its feet and loped off into the desert. He thought to wonder about its destination, but his state of being prevented it. It was his third day without food, and his stomach had given up hope of fullness.

Instead, his mental faculties had slowed, and he operated more and more from a space of instinct. He noted the sky overhead. Blue, no chance of rain. No chance of cloud cover either. The air – it was cool. There had been a shift in the night and the relentless spring warmth had dwindled. He scanned the sky again – had he missed something? No, just blue. Just the pure azure reality of the sky above the sand that connected heaven and earth in some realm known only to the winged creatures.

He recalled his dream – He had flown over the earth and he had seen the union of tame and wild. He had seen his companion merge with the wilderness, and he had longed to join. Here he was, in the sand, awake and contemplating. Few thoughts crossed his mind. It was more a stream of disconnected notions than consciousness. We won't be eating today, he thought. It didn't occur to him that he spoke only for himself but did so as a plurality.

He rose, brushed the sand from his clothes, his hair, his skin, and drank deeply from the river, placing his lips to the surface of the water like some beast slurping sustenance from the earth. Then he stood and walked without thought to the juniper. And there he sat for several hours – how many he couldn't be sure.

He watched the shadows move across the desert floor, felt the heat of the day grow overhead. But still there was a chill in the air that held the sun at bay. The dog trotted in and out of view. Once, Joseph stood – for what reason he wasn't sure – and scanned the horizon.

He observed the dog leaping forward, seizing a rabbit, and devouring it. It stood as it ate, an imposing figure above the helpless, eviscerated smaller animal.

The boy found himself repulsed. How can one take life so needlessly, he thought? He saw the dog in its most primal, carnivorous state, and he found himself drawing back. The animal was all-consumed by the work; absorbed in its feast. It didn't care if the boy looked on – probably it didn't even notice. But the boy noticed the beast. He saw it had changed, and he found himself fearful.

Night. Back at the camp. Thoughts were by now fewer than a couple of words long. He thought in terms of spaces and tangible things. Where he was. What was before him. What he needed in the moment. If he was cold, his only thought was as such. Perhaps he would consider a remedy, but these strings of pragmatic process were primordial and simple.

He found himself lying on his back, a fire glowing beside him, his body comfortable, his eyes fixed on the heavens above. It was as though he were one with the stars overhead. How sparse the separation between him and them. He was sure he saw the sky pulse with a heartbeat. The stars themselves seemed to move in time. A voice spoke to him from the beyond but he couldn't understand what it said. Still, the melody soothed him, and he began drifting in and out of sleep.

In his hunger, his reality had begun to take on a dreamlike tinge. The lights and colors and sounds of his desert world merged into a stream of sensory input hardly distinguishable and increasingly less meaningful. He felt himself growing weaker, more lethargic, but he did not fight it. He wondered if he was indeed surrendering to death, but kept feeling the pulse in his neck, and telling himself that he was simply embracing the experience of becoming one with the desert.

While he slept, vivid flashes of past lives came to him once again.

Dreams of past loves. Dreams of Mary, of Madeline. Dreams of his first death in the desert. Dreams of the man with the black braids and infinite wisdom. Dreams of vultures circling. Dreams of death. He awoke in the night dripping with sweat, a wretched taste in his mouth, but fell back into sleep quickly.

Restless, fitful. Nothing made sense. All was a blur. The lines between waking and dreaming grew increasingly thin.

He saw the moon overhead, it was blinding. Still, the river lulled him. Sand was uncomfortable, but he found the layers beneath the surface cool, and the comfort discovered by his hands in their mindless burrowing soothed him enough to nod back off.

He found the dog, too, in his fitfulness. It had curled up next to him again, and again his hands found its fur. His companion; his safest refuge and his greatest threat.

He dreamed it was standing over him, devouring his heart.

He awoke with a start, staring into the blackness of the trees. An owl overhead, hooting. Looking around.

Back to sleep. No dreams. Just blackness

Day 4

Sun high overhead. Hot; sweat.

The hunger inside him had transformed into a sleeping beast, quiet but fearsome, and he wondered when it would awaken to tear him apart. Any shred of cool had left in the night like a thief, leaving only a sweltering day. Had it been yesterday when he woke to a chill in the air? He couldn't be certain.

The dog had gone. The owl, too. His mind flashed to waking in the night with it sitting overhead, hooting its ghostly call.

It felt late in the morning. The sun blinding on its celestial perch, the shadows it cast indicating a higher position.

He sat up. The river. Sand. Sand in every crease of skin. Sand in his mouth.

I should sleep on my back, he thought.

He undressed and waded into the river. The cool water cleansed the dust from his body and brought a brief clarity to his mind. A dull ache in his stomach. The same foul taste in his mouth. He felt his face and found his skin sunken across his cheekbones. The beginnings of a scraggy beard across his chin.

He splashed the holy water over his shoulder, across his chest, droplets streaming down his stomach in murky rivers like tears on the face of a dirty child. He thought of Gabriel and wondered how he was. Does he worry about me? Do I worry about him? Thoughts were disconnected.

After a while he sat in the river, the water up to his neck. He leaned back and let it wash over him utterly. The sounds of water like voices down a distant, reverberant hallway flooded his ears. The wild pulsed within him, though its power was feeble. He felt more like an ancient vista than a raging sea.

He opened his eyes and stared up at the waves of light filtering through the water above. The need for breath began to claw at his chest, but he felt inclined to deny it. As he exhaled the pent-up carbon-dioxide in broad bubbles scampering to the surface, he sank lower. The current tousled his hair, the river's song lulling him.

Eventually the pain in his lungs seared so heartily that his will to live urged him upward. He broke from the water and gulped at the air. It was hot and dry inside him and he felt like a vast, empty container.

We believe we are so important, he thought. We structure our lives and construct cities and go about for a hundred years doing mostly nothing. But perhaps we are just vessels, filled with the elements of the wild, animated by God for no reason in particular.

He waded to the shore and sat naked in the sand. His gaze soft across the horizon. Sun baked his skin. He felt as though he'd just experienced a rebirth. Except instead of being delivered into a bright, offensive reality, he had been born into a despondent stoicism from which he merely watched the world without having much opinion at all.

It occurred to him to go look for the dog. It wasn't that he worried, or needed the companionship, but he thought it a suitable activity to watch another living thing for a time. He set off across the sand, the heat from the midday sun rising in waves of iridescence. The whole desert was like a dream. It hadn't occurred to him to dress. He noticed the sun on his bare skin.

After what felt like much longer than normal, he reached the juniper and sat, his back leaning against its flaking bark. The tree so sturdy, its skin so soft and pliable. A suitable spot to spend the rest of eternity.

The dog appeared a bit later, a streak crossing the desert in pursuit of another rabbit. He was taken by the muscular stature of the animal, which seemed to have bloomed overnight. Ears forward, head low, shoulders pulsing forward in great bounds. A leap, a snap of jaws and a noiseless death to an animal raised by the desert to sustain its predators.

He recalled the dream in which he had seen the dog join with the wolves. He could see the wild beasts within his companion now, and he began to understand.

Joseph looked on as the victor reveled. He was both fascinated and repulsed. Trickles of crimson ran from the dog's mouth as it tore flesh from bone. A merciless transformation from one life into another. He could almost taste the blood of the prey, feel the life energy pulsing through his own body. The dog ate without regard for possible interruption. Above, a crow circled, eyeing the feast with the look of a beggar.

Here we are in this dance, thought the boy, where all that lives does so only to nourish the earth. But do we only nourish the earth in our dying, he wondered? Can we also nourish the earth through our living?

Then, as though the warm flesh and blood of the dog's kill sank into his own stomach, he grew suddenly weary and lay back against the tree to doze.

It was dark when he awoke, and cold. He thought to move back to their camp by the river, so that he could at least put on his clothes, but shrugged off his discomfort with the lethargy of a dying man. The dog had bedded down with him again, besides, and he turned to it for warmth. Sleep came again and this time, stayed till morning.

Day 5

It was before dawn when the waking world found him. He had slept through early morning the last few days and he was awed by the unfamiliar dawn, the color of the sky, and the quiet presence of a few bold stars.

All around, life was still. The boy, too, was still. Not just his body, but his entire being. His breath was gentle, hardly perceptible, his heartbeat patient and thoughtful. Even his thoughts held a certain reverence. All was quiet, at rest.

He observed his surroundings. Sky overhead, pin-holed with points of light calling and beckoning him to join their astral existence.

Sand below, juniper behind. Inside him, nothing.

Breath – was he breathing? Perhaps death had come and heaven had revealed itself to be an identical life on some other plane where breath is but a myth.

There was a dryness in his mouth but his mind could not grasp the concept long enough to act. He blinked, his eyes as dry.

Moving was work, raising himself from the sand a nearly impossible task. When he got to his feet the world spun and he returned to sitting.

There he stayed, staring blankly out at the vivid landscape until the sun was high and the urge for hydration overcame the struggle of attaining it.

His head pounded. His stomach cramped as though shards of glass filled his abdomen.

Stumbling to the river, stumbling into it.

The water washed him and again called him back to life. He gulped at the current until his belly ached.

Crawling to the bank. Finally reaching sand, collapsing into it.

He awoke and the sun was low on the western horizon. Long shadows and a deadly silence loomed. He rolled onto his back and stared upward at the tree. The owl had returned.

"A little early for you, isn't it," he said aloud. His voice startled him amidst the silent wild. The sound shook him, but more the rasp with which he spoke. He felt near death, scarcely strong enough to persist with the beating of his quiet heart.

For a brief, fleeting instant, logic crossed his mind and he understood that people had gone much longer without food. He would not die in the desert.

He thought to drink more – or rather his instincts dragged his ragged frame to the water. With the coolness coursing through him, he found himself sitting at the bank, the river lapping at his toes. He still had not dressed and he could feel the chill-hot tightness of sunburn on his back and neck.

He stared across the river to the red land beyond. For a moment he thought he saw a man walk across his field of vision. A tall, strong man – confident.

But the images were short-lived, and the man vanished without a trace.

Joseph blinked, rubbing his eyes. He looked again but saw nothing. Then another movement from the corner of his eye. He looked, but again saw nothing. Perplexed and intrigued, he marshalled his strength and set out to see what he could. He walked in slow, labored steps, stopping every few to survey the desert.

He saw no human, no beast, except the occasional glimpse of the dog off in the neighborhood of the juniper, engaged in its perpetual play. He walked on. Still nothing. He walked for so long he forgot he was walking, and when he turned around, he could hardly see the river.

A fleeting pang of panic shot through him. Finding himself so unexpectedly far from water, from familiarity, from the only place he could now consider anything like home – though he knew it was a far cry from a real home – jolted him; broke something loose within.

He had become untethered to anything of meaning, and he was overcome by a flood of emotion. All the weight of the last nine months found him at once. It had been chasing him down, and he'd been outrunning it. But here, deep in the belly of the arid, sun-drenched precipice, it caught him, and it seized him utterly.

Alone amidst an enormous and unforgiving world, Joseph wept heartily. In his despondence and disjointed thought, he had forgotten the weight of feeling. It overwhelmed him, and he sat in the sand, naked against a crimson sun, heaving great sobs. His tears left dimples in the sand.

He wept for the aimlessness of a man without a purpose. He wept for the loves he had mishandled in his blindness. For the loves he had overlooked or left behind as he staggered on in search of himself. He wept because life was cruel, and because it was difficult, and because nothing good ever seemed to last. He wept because his childhood had been stolen from him, and because he was alone.

He was alone. The thought quieted his mind. He was alone, but he was alive.

As quickly as it had come, the tempest in his heart subsided. He drew a great breath of the dry evening air. The world reels after a rainstorm, aghast at the cleansing waves that break and recede without warning. Joseph became as still, and felt as clean.

He looked out; his senses sharpened by baptismal tears. The sky the most vivid violet, the sand a complimentary pink, the green of the sage a soft sweep of hair across the face of a beautiful woman. He thought of Mary.

How lovely was the presence of a woman. And for the first time, he felt the same kinship and comfort from the desert around him. The soft breeze kissed his neck and ruffled his hair. The heat emanating from the sand under him wrapped him in an embrace. The perfume of juniper smoke filled his nostrils and he closed his eyes, breathing deep in reverence.

But how had there been smoke if not a fire?

He looked again and was seated before a fire, modest in size but healthy and crackling. Beside him his fire implements, his drill and its base, warm from their work. He did not recall starting the fire, but his hands bled from their labor. Perhaps, he thought, it is better not to ask questions.

So there he sat as the twilight grew around him. The fire warmed him where the night grew chill, and in his awareness there stood a new clarity. Thoughts still came and went in a sporadic stream of disconnected concepts, but there was a beating pulse in his veins that propelled him forward in time and space like the ticking of some immaculate clock.

He saw in the flames the faces of Gabriel, and Sam and Sister Anna. He gave thanks for their role in his life. Then he put more wood on the fire.

Day 6

How glorious is rest, he thought as the blanket of sleep was pulled from his body by the coming day. He breathed deeply, the smell of the morning filling him.

He rose and stretched and noticed a new and surprising strength within himself.

Walking back to the river, he was astonished to recount how far he'd wandered the previous evening. He gave thanks, too, that he had not wandered further, or walked off the edge of a canyon in his daze. Perhaps the desert really was some divine mother who held every intention of keeping him safe.

When he got to the river he drank his fill. Looking up, water beading on his face and dripping from his beard, he saw the dog sitting on the far bank, watching him. They stood for a moment as statues, gazes locked and unwavering. Perhaps he wants to eat me, he thought. He remembered the dream in which it stood over him, devouring his heart.

But he did not feel threatened – he felt more alive than he ever had. He leapt into motion, springing himself forward in the direction of the dog.

It jumped back as the boy landed on the bank, surprised but eager to engage. It lowered its head, rump raised, tail wagging. Another leap forward, this time far enough to land atop the animal.

Joseph felt his own weakness in sharp contrast to the dog's strength. Still, they wrestled, chasing each other around the shady sand beneath the cottonwood. Great whoops and guttural growls emanated from the playfulness. He felt the crows overhead watching, confused.

After a time, the dog broke out against the arid terrain in a full sprint. Suddenly alone, the boy sat, catching his breath. A spark lived in his soul and he felt light, effortless as the breeze.

After a while, the dog trotted back with a rabbit in its mouth. A hunger roared inside, and the rabbit drew his interest. He had no other thought but to sink his teeth into the creature, to feel its flesh inside of him, to savor the warmth of life and draw nourishment from it.

He stepped towards the dog, who had begun to devour its prey. But to Joseph's surprise, the animal raised its eyes slightly and growled a fearsome growl. Hackles raised, an imposing figure over its catch, the full power of the beast came into full view.

Joseph raised his hands and stepped back. He sat in the sand and watched. But his hunger had been awakened, and it began to gnaw at him.

That afternoon, he tried to catch his own, but his speed was no match for the rabbits he chased, and he grew more and more weary with each attempt. Eventually, he returned to the river, unsuccessful and aching everywhere from overexertion.

He gulped at the water and set about building a fire. The warmth lulled him to sleep at once. Once again, his dreaming returned.

He saw himself sitting on a slab of stone, legs crossed, hair disheveled. His face was thin, but stoic. He couldn't tell whether he stared ahead through squinted eyes or if the eyelids were closed. There was a blankness about him.

The wind began to whip, and he began to spin. Round and round his body he moved, seeing his seated position from all angles. The wind intensified, and seemed to scream through the nearby canyons. Sand was blowing in all directions, lodging in his hair, between his lips, in his ears. Still, the figure below – his own body – didn't budge. The stillness of the boy he saw startled him.

His hair was blowing fiercely, and all at once it began to come undone. Whisps blew from his head like smoke off a dirty flame. Then skin. He watched in muted horror as his own body began to blow away like some inanimate sculpture of sand and smoke.

He saw his clothes begin to fray, and eventually unravel. They seemed to melt like ice in a flame, pouring off his body in great rivers of thread, disappearing as they left the security of the larger garment.

Then his skin. In much the same way, it seemed to transform into microscopic grains, blowing off his pointed shoulders and bony, seated hips the same way sand blows off the top of a dune.

The wind blew ever stronger, and his remains were scant. As the skin blew from his bones in crumbling clouds of dust, he discovered that nothing existed beneath his ribs. No substance could be found of his innards, but rather a great hollow void, giving way to the great unbecoming.

Not even a heart remained in the cavity of his chest, and before long, the wild and wicked wind had taken everything and all that remained of the boy's body was the knife which had been fastened in his belt.

He watched as it sat there, teetering on the slab as the wind tried to lift it and carry it off, too. But the knife was too heavy, too unbreakable, and eventually the wind grew tired of trying and set off to some other far-flung destination.

Then, quiet. All was quiet. So painfully, utterly quiet. And where was he? He watched, still, but he was gone. His soul had become one with the desert, and his final experience as a man had been to watch his own body be blown to pieces by the merciless wind.

He felt... nothing. In his new experience there was no joy, no peace, no sorrow, no pain. There was neither longing nor having. Certainly, there was action, movement, the loyal obedience of the creatures to the whim of the earth, but no thought accompanied the witness. Only noticing without preference and without judgement. Yet, somewhere in this strange and vivid land, there existed an emptiness which tasted a bit like regret and felt inside him like disappointment.

Then, as though he were a child backing away from something horrible, Joseph found himself staggering backwards, shaking his head violently and muttering the words "No, No, No," over and over again.

In an instant, he felt cold water consume him. In his sleep he had crawled from his resting place in the sand and found himself in the river, the swift, cool water up to his neck.

The cold shook him to consciousness and he came to understand that the vision from which he'd just emerged was only a dream. A horrid dream, a nightmare. But perhaps a message as well.

He clawed his way back to the bank and heaved his soaking body onto the sand. There he lay, staring up at the bright morning overhead, the sun still below the hills to the east. He shivered in the cool of the eager dawn and, before long, slipped back into sleep, not to awaken until the sun was near its zenith.

Day 7

His waking came with startling swiftness. In an instant he was alive and staring up at the tree.

I need to eat, he thought. I will not die in the desert – It is time to claim life once again and to leave this place.

Rising and donning his clothes for the first time in several days – more so as protection against the relentless sun than for the sake of decency – he set off in search of food.

The events of the day before – had it been the day before? – and his dream that morning seemed to have awakened in him a specific alertness with which he now saw the desert. It was as though everything around him were present for the sole purpose of directing him, leading him towards life.

He had heard that life always finds life, and this notion offered reassurance that he would not perish amidst the vacant, endless sands. Watching the sky overhead, he took note of the crows engaged in their usual laborious play.

Returning his gaze to the landscape before him, he noted the green snake of the river's foliage to his right and the far-distant foothills from which the river emanated. He was contemplating faint, sandy impressions resembling hoofprints when he saw a large shadow cross the ground before him. Looking skyward he saw an enormous bird soaring, motionless atop invisible currents. Moving his gaze laterally he noticed more, some way off, circling.

Buzzards. He recalled the tales he'd heard of buzzards circling the remains of some dead or dying beast, and it occurred to him that perhaps he could find the meal these winged reapers now stalked from the skies.

He began to walk. His direction certain, he moved more quickly than an emaciated boy should have been able. Then he saw it, but at first didn't believe. Atop the sand some five hundred feet off was a heap of flesh and fur. Perhaps it is just an illusion of the desert, no different than the man I thought I saw previously, he thought.

But as he drew closer and the image didn't evaporate, his body began to respond to the promise of food. A primal ferocity overtook him and he ran to the carcass. Crouching over his find, giving brief gratitude to the desert for his deliverance, he pulled the knife from his belt.

The stench was nearly overwhelming, but the prospect of nourishment clouded his judgement. He tore through the skin and fur, cutting out chunks of muscle. It was warm, which he mistook to mean the animal had suffered a recent death. In fact, it was the sun that had half-baked the carcass over the span of several days.

He ate mercilessly. The meat filled him quickly and he wiped the blood from his face with his shirt.

With reddened hands and a glutton's weariness he fell back in the sand, resting his head upon the bare rock on which he lay.

The sun was blinding, and he closed his eyes.

Before he drifted into a bizarre rest, overcome with sudden exhaustion and light-headedness, he thought to move from the exposure of the slab, but sleep came too quickly.

In an instant he was awake. The baking sun was high overhead, and a fiery intensity roared from his middle.

He rolled over just in time to spew a bloody spray over the sandstone. He had been on the brink of dehydration before vomiting, and the violent expulsion of his poisonous meal had drained his last reserves of water.

He knew the consequences of failing to rehydrate and scanned the horizon for the river. It was perhaps a half-mile off, but in his muscles there existed no strength.

Still, he made an earnest effort to rise and began to stumble and claw his way towards the bounty of green in the distance.

Walking was impossible work, and he ached in every inch of his body. He stumbled frequently, sand and sage infiltrating his mouth and nose as he scrambled through grimy dust clouds of his own making.

The only thought in his mind was water.

His vision began to grow cloudy, his head began to spin, and he crashed to the ground.

On hands and knees, shaking all over, he dry-heaved as his wretched stomach tried in vain to gain equilibrium.

All went black as he fell face-first in the burning sand.

It was a blindingly bright day when he finally regained consciousness. A crystalline whiteness emanated from the sky and a cool breeze blew against the heat of the sun. Once his eyes adjusted to the glare he saw standing before him the man from his visions, his desert guide, his teacher from some different and powerful world. Next to him sat the dog. The man was petting the dogs head, scratching behind his ears, but the dog seemed aloof to the attention. Both figures stared fixedly upon the boy, and the man smiled almost imperceptibly.

"Who are you?" Joseph asked half in anger and half in astonishment.

"That's not so important."

"But I keep seeing you and I need to know why."

"Who are you?" The man asked in response.

"You know who I am," he said, but the man just stared at him, waiting. "I am Joseph. I am a boy in the desert, on the brink of death. Again."

"Again." The man said, and the smile disappeared from his face. He looked almost sorrowful.

Joseph detested the pity the man seemed to express with his eyes.

"I chose to come out here. I chose this. I needed this."

"Why?" asked the man.

"You should know. You seem to appear to me every time I approach some sort of death."

"But do you know why?"

"No. Maybe. I had never felt so alive as when I emerged from the desert last autumn. But life in the town felt like slowly dying, so I came out here in search of life. I only knew to find it in the desert."

"And have you found what you were looking for?"

Joseph paused. He looked at his hands, still stained in the blood of his failed feasting. His stomach held a haunting emptiness.

"Today I feel closer to death than I ever have."

The man smiled. "Then perhaps it's today that you are ready to begin to live again."

"But how? How can I live when I cannot eat? I doubt I will even survive to make it back to the river to drink. I'm beginning to think the buzzards were there for me."

The man chuckled. Then he was silent for a time, staring at Joseph with a mixture of expectation and compassion. After a while, he spoke, and as he did, he laid his hand to rest on the dog's head.

"Reap the bounty of the desert. Everything you need is already within reach."

☽

Joseph was jolted awake by a tugging at his pant leg. The dog had come to find him and was frantically attempting to rouse him.

Animals always know when another is close to death, he thought. He sat up, mustering all his strength, and spoke in a feeble yet reassuring tone to the animal. It licked his face and he scratched its neck affectionately.

"Alright, we're going to take this slow, but we're going to make it to the river."

He rose cautiously and wiped the dried chunks of meat from his shirt and hands. One step at a time, he made his way down the interminable path to the safety and respite of the riverbed.

It seemed impossible that he had actually arrived. He sat on the river's bank for a long moment before stooping to slurp at its edge. After drinking modestly he splashed his face. His head pounded and his stomach wasn't altogether pleased with its contents. Still he felt the hope of survival within his bones, and he made careful work of regaining his strength.

For hours upon hours, he alternated between reclining against a nearby cottonwood and drinking measured sips from the babbling water. The sun traversed its path through the sky, the shadows growing long. By nightfall he had quieted the raging beast inside him, and though immensely weak and ragged, he felt a steady determination that had eluded him until that point. He slept deeply and with neither dream nor fitfulness.

Day 8

Alone in the preemptive heat of early morning, he recalled what the man had said and wondered if perhaps the dog would be his salvation after all – or at least until they escaped this arid purgatory of rebirth.

He stood and walked from the riverbed, scanning the horizon for the dog. He caught sight of it just as it sprung forward in pursuit of its next meal – his next meal. He approached, and again the animal raised its eyes, growling. But this time Joseph didn't immediately back off. He stood his ground and gazed directly into its eyes.

Now his ferocity, his embodied wilderness, matched that of the animal. He felt no need to retreat. Instead he took another step closer, so that he was only a foot or so away from the animal. He crouched on one knee. And there they stayed for an endless instant, eyes locked in a battle of will and dominance, each unwilling to fall back the rabbit still beneath the dog's front paw their prize. Steady and unyielding, Joseph stayed where he was. Eventually the dog's snarl relaxed into a mild rumble and its hackles lowered.

Joseph inched closer and stretched out his hand. The dog remained immobile, frozen for that brief eternity in its position of cautious submission. And then Joseph, eyes still locked with the dog's, reached forward and picked up the rabbit. The dog lay down and stared at Joseph intently, but without aggression. Drawing the knife from his belt, he removed the hind quarters from the rabbit and lay the rest of the still-warm mammal at the dog's front feet.

"I appreciate you, friend," he said to the dog, and patted it on the head.

The two sat in the sand, eating their modest meal in silence, each intently pulling flesh from bone with claws and teeth.

He marveled at the way the nourishment pulsed immediately within him. All the life with which the rabbit had attempted to escape its pursuer was now flowing in the blood of Joseph himself. How different this fresh meat felt inside him. The carrion he'd consumed earlier – which his body had immediately expelled – had felt hot, heavy, and agonizing. But this... this filled him with an energy that awakened every sense, seemed to open every capillary in his body. He felt his awareness growing, expanding, such that the sounds and sights that met him illuminated in a vast and elaborate tapestry. The wind across every grain of sand, the river over every stone, the juniper and premature sage tickling the sky from their earthbound bed. Every movement of the desert was within him – was him – and to notice these things was to live them first-hand.

A new breath filled his lungs, and he found himself party to a new clarity and purposefulness. Vivid vitality, moments before but a myth, now defined his existence. Joseph and the dog stayed seated across from each other, bloodied sand and remnants of a furry pelt between them, until late in the afternoon. It was then he knew the time had come to leave. He had entered the desert little more than a week prior, but many lifetimes had come and gone. Reborn and renewed, more grounded and wilder than ever, the time had come to seek the next adventure.

"Time to go, my friend," Joseph said to his companion, and the two rose and began walking.

The vast expanse of desert through which they ambled drew up at its edges like a great dish upon which the most exquisite flavors of the earth were to be served. Sky arched overhead in a miasma of scattered, wispy clouds that threatened rain. Against the heat, the unexpected humidity brought Joseph to sweating.

Their walk was a somber one, if not for their escape from death, then because they were indeed each leaving a wild, untamed piece of themselves behind as they went forth to join once again the civilized world. How can we live in both realities, Joseph wondered? How do we walk with one foot in each world, neither forsaking our wildness nor shunning our humanity? These thoughts and others lilted in and out of his mind as he and the dog carried on at a leisurely pace towards their unknown destination.

By late afternoon, after they'd followed the green, flowering snake of the river, the edges of their cosmic plate began to lift upwards. Flowing sandstone peaked here and there, the remnants of some long-ago sea.

The entire landscape bore the impressions of ancient water. Rock and sky and shrub and sand all merged effortlessly with the other, each bringing such intricate depth to the surreal portraiture that on several occasions, walking amongst the stationary deluge gave the boy a sense of vertigo.

It was the magical hour of evening by the time they reached the mouth of a canyon. Growing increasingly narrow, the river chipping away day after day, year after year, carving its home from the solid stone, the walls hung high overhead framing a surrealist sky.

In the waning light, the features and curvature of the sandstone became like fingerprints of imperfect divinity. Joseph ran his hand along the curves seeing them through all his senses.

After a time, the two came to a place where there existed a sandy bank. The walls surrounding were hollowed like a drinking bowl and marvelously smooth. He began gathering a modest pile of driftwood that had accumulated from the spring's heavy rains. Before long, a small fire was burning, its smoke curling up towards the heavens, caressing the sandstone with the same tender touch the boy had expressed to the canyon earlier in the afternoon.

It was early evening. The trickle of water reverberated off the canyon walls, making it feel to Joseph as though he were under water. The light, too, echoed as it only ever does in a deep sandstone chasm, and when it finally fell upon the sand on which he sat, there was a blue tint that hinted at early darkness.

He lay back. The journey ahead was still shrouded in mystery. Perhaps the canyon in which they now wandered would terminate at a waterfall too high or sheer for them to traverse, and they'd have to wander back out until they reached the desert again. Or perhaps they would become trapped in a sudden flood typical of the region and time of year.

But perhaps – and it was the possibility of success that enticed him to the point of carrying on in spite of his uncertainty – perhaps they would hike for a while through this dream-like visage and emerge unto another world, this time closer to a place they could call home.

His mind wandered. The emptiness and hunger inside him gnawed, having been awakened but not slaked. Still, a sureness inside his heart quelled panic.

That night, as he lay atop the sandy bank in the bosom of the canyon, an infant lying in wait for birth amidst the comfort of familiar warmth, he dreamed a potent dream. It was one of those dreams that brings into question the plausibility of life itself as something separate from the imaginary.

He was standing, and before him was a woman. She looked up at him and an unyielding love emanated from her gaze. He held her face in his hands and admired her eyes, which pierced him utterly with both a ferocity and gentleness.

Around them, the world spun on in some iteration of chaos, but he paid it no mind.

She was supple, not necessarily in a physical sense, but more so the way a baby radiates possibility and surrender to the eventuality of the life it is destined to lead.

She was young. Younger than many of the women he'd known. She reminded him of Mary. But she was more assured than Mary had been and he trusted her deeply.

The way she looked at him made him feel a power and responsibility that was at once foreign and familiar. As he held her face in his hands, he held his entire world, and hers as well.

He kissed her forehead and she closed her eyes, drinking him in. They released. His vision widened. He saw their children run into her arms, looking back at him as they did and smiling as broadly as though they could have no other wish than to be exactly where they were.

It was the first time he'd dreamed of children. But there they were. They followed him with smiling eyes as he sat down in the grass. They were on a hill, overlooking a forest. There was such peace, such richness. He felt a blooming in his heart.

His dream continued as his body began to rouse. He resisted the waking, not wanting to leave the vision which had brought him so much fullness. She came to his side and rested her head on his shoulder. Together they watched their children run down the hill, giggling, tumbling and landing eventually upon their backs in a heap of laughter and joy.

But the desert beckoned. It called him back to life.

As he closed his eyes there on that hill, the love of his life in the crook of his arm with her head on his chest, he returned to the vivid austerity of the sandstone womb in which he lay.

He stared upward at the sky, pinpricked with light, the stars tinkling like bells against the canyon wall. It was not morning. No glow pushed at the edges of the stone above, indicating night's departure. He breathed deeply, otherwise unmoving.

What had he seen? Who was she?

Thoughts of her sent chills up his spine. He closed his eyes, and images of her flooded back through him. He saw her walking alongside him, her summer dress ruffling golden stalks of grass growing down some dirt path. He saw her sleeping in the hopeful light of morning, her hair across the pillow like a bridal train, and just as stunning. He felt her hand in his. Her lips on his lips. Her body against his own. It was as though the cells of his being realigned as she moved closer.

Again he opened his eyes and found himself in the desert.

A goodness filled his chest with each breath, and he recognized within him a knowing. She was out there. He knew she had been made for him, and he for her. He didn't know where to find her, or how. But he had found a point towards which to orient his heart's compass, and he trusted the world to guide him there.

His chest heaved a greedy gulp of crisp, dry oxygen. Her face flashed before his mind's eye. He lingered there, gazing into her eyes, fierce with fury and glowing with the uninhibited spark of youthful optimism. She was breathtaking. The tangible passion that passed through her hands into him told stories of the wildness he felt within his own soul. He had never seen her face before this dream, and yet she was immediately familiar.

The dog, which had roused slightly and lay looking at him through half-awake eyes, fell back asleep. The boy lay looking up at the heavens. He was far removed from his body, walking among the fields of a golden sunset, hand in hand with her. The smile resting on his lips quivered as she kissed him.

Visions are wonderful things, he thought, as he noticed the first light of dawn rising over the eastern wall. But one day, it will be this night that exists only in my heart, and she will be there resting on my shoulder, as real as the sand on which I sit and the sun which rises over that ridge.

He sat up, suddenly impelled to depart in pursuit of his next chapter. His time in the desert had come to an end.

He knew where he was going – or if perhaps not where, at least to whom – and so he packed camp, and set off in search of this mysterious woman who had transformed him in one, simple, solitary night.

Part 4

In a small but growing town called La Villa, there stood a chapel. This chapel had been the pride and joy of the sisters who had worked tirelessly to bring it to fruition. And as it neared completion, it became clear that it really would be an incredible work of architecture and a fitting testament to their love of God.

But in the last days, a simple question had unearthed something problematic. By some unfortunate and incredible oversight, nobody had factored in a staircase to access the choir loft. Now an afterthought, it became apparent to the builders that any staircase great enough to access the mezzanine, which stood over eighteen feet above the floor, would have rendered the nave too narrow to hold the congregation. A traditional staircase would have blocked some of the stained-glass windows, or blocked the center aisle, or taken the space required by half of the pews. All of this lent an air of defeat to the otherwise joyous final stages of the project.

One nun was unfazed, however. Sister Matilde, who enjoyed a benevolent position at the head of the convent, was a devout woman. She always stood very straight, but her wry humor often betrayed her true character. So when the rest of the cloister sisters descended into weeping madness over the tragedy of their unfinishable chapel, it was Sister Matilde who calmed them down.

Over their evening meal, she quieted them for a moment and spoke to them of faith. She related her own curiosity at how their current conundrum might unfold, but displayed not a single thread of doubt. This was easy for her to do, because she was the sort of woman who hadn't doubted the presence of God in her life for even a moment since the day she was born.

The other sisters perceived her calm and resolve, and it settled their hearts just enough that when she suggested they sit that night after supper in a congregate prayer, they agreed.

Sister Matilde's position would have precluded any outward dissent, but all the sisters had nonetheless agreed that her wisdom was most likely correct and appropriate. So that night, they all sat together in the very chapel about which they sought reassurance, and they prayed.

The next morning the nuns all ran to the chapel, each of them hoping to find their miracle had been performed. When they saw that the room appeared exactly as it had the night before, they became visibly defeated.

But Sister Matilde strode into the room full of disconcerted nuns, and she asked them if it wasn't a beautiful day to be alive. Mary Alice and probably others wondered what Matilde knew that they didn't, because she seemed too cheerful - too unfazed by the lack of immediate resolution. But Matilde told them nothing, for indeed there was nothing to tell, and eventually they all went on with their day as usual.

Except that there had been something that Sister Matilde knew that was known only to her. The previous night she had had a dream. In her dream an angle of the lord had appeared to her, and it had simply smiled. From her encounter she had felt such warmth, such reassurance, and she knew somehow that this angel had been sent to her in order to reassure her that her faith was not unfounded. But since the angel hadn't spoken, she saw it fitting to likewise remain silent, and to exude the same positivity she had seen upon the angel's face as she went about her day.

Sister Matilde was the sort of person who seemed able to accept the messages in her life without worry or consternation.

Eight more days passed, and the sisters of the convent had begun to accept that theirs would be a chapel with a beautiful balcony from which only the angels themselves could sing. All except for Sister Matilde, who had remained buoyant in her certainty that a miracle was indeed on its way.

On the ninth day a man came into the town with a bundle of tools on the back of a mule. He wore a hearty beard and was dressed in humble clothes, but in his eyes there glimmered something of another story.

When he walked into town, he happened to walk straight through the busy Saturday streets to the front steps of the chapel, which is where and when he met Sister Matilde. It appeared to those who witnessed the meeting that Sister Matilde had been waiting for him. When he approached, she smiled warmly and received him as though he were an old friend. The truth was that they had never met, and she had only come to the steps to fetch something for one of the other sisters. But as soon as she walked through the doors, she had forgotten what it was.

When she saw the man approaching with his mule and simple shoes, she smiled because she thought he looked just like Jesus entering Jerusalem. Still, the whole scene flowed with so much predestination that the man's origins – along with his possible previous ties to Sister Matilde, and his purpose for coming to town – became something that many people talked about, even though there really was nothing to it.

His name was Abram and it seemed everyone he met liked him immediately. But perhaps the one who seemed to like him most of all was Sister Matilde, because within two minutes of stepping foot in the chapel, he not only noticed the missing stairs but promised a solution as well. After learning from the sisters where he might water his mule, he departed with a tip of his hat and a promise that he would return later that evening to graciously accept their offer of a good, hot supper.

By the time he had returned, he'd washed and pulled his beard into a tight bun under his chin such that he resembled a Persian king. In his hand when he approached the steps was a rolled sheet of paper, on which was drawn a very detailed set of plans for a staircase unlike anything they had ever seen.

Instead of ascending the space in a linear direction, his proposed staircase spiraled upwards so that its footprint took scarcely any space at all. Most mesmerizing was that this drawing seemed to imply that Abram could build it without any supports, neither down the middle nor around the edges, which until he suggested it, no one had thought possible.

Everyone who saw the plans thought the design incredible. And for a while there was a kind of simple hope inhabiting the sisters that only comes when amazing and unexpected solutions manifest themselves to life's most daunting challenges.

The architects and builders of the chapel took one look at the drawings and said it couldn't be done. The wood available in their part of the country wouldn't work. Besides, no man on his own could build such a structure let alone erect it within the ribs of the already-built church. But Abram smiled simply in the face of their doubts and agreed to start as soon as Sister Matilde gave him permission.

He would not discuss any compensation for his labor, nor payment for materials, in spite of Sister Matilde's urgings, but he did accept a small room with two beds in the chapel itself. The room had been reserved for the traveling priests, and Abram agreed only once he was assured they wouldn't be coming to visit until the chapel was done anyway.

After the agreement had been made, Abram seemed to disappear. But on his bed he left his set of tools minus his timber saw, and Sister Matilde made it clear that he was to be expected back at any time, and that his room should not be disturbed.

Over the following month, as the air was beginning to warm and the spring weather brought the rare moisture that everything depended on, Abram became something of a fixture in the town. All of it felt like the blooming of something new, and it became difficult to find a conversation amongst the people that did not in some way mention the old carpenter.

Every few days, he would return with enormous logs in tow behind his mule. This was peculiar because the trees in the area surrounding the town were all small in girth or twisted in the trunk. And those who had never left the area had never seen trees so large. Never mind how he'd managed to fell, hitch and haul them on his own. It all left many questions.

The children would run from their homes or from the shops on the main streets no matter the time of day and ask the man about where he'd been and what he was doing. And in response, he gave the children comical answers that played on their wild imaginations, only adding to the mystery surrounding his existence.

Only Sister Matilde knew what he was up to, but she seemed humored by the air of intrigue around the town's most-discussed stranger as much as Abram himself, so she kept her information guarded behind a sly smile and sparkling eyes.

It was a surprisingly hot day in May when Joseph wandered into the town, still gaunt and sunburned from his time in the desert.

At his heels trotted the dog with black fur and pointed ears, which many in the town agreed resembled more closely a wolf than a dog. He carried with him no possessions, which made him appear suspicious, since people tend to doubt that happiness is possible without material comforts.

But Joseph paid these whisperings no mind, and he may not have noticed them at all. As he walked through the new town, he was busy seeing it with eyes new to him, and he couldn't help but find himself taken by every little detail. But it wasn't just the things in the town that caught his attention; it was the people too. And when he saw them he smiled more genuinely than they were used to. And that made them distrust him all the more.

He walked past a square where old men played chess at tables set up on the plaza and thought that perhaps he would one day sit among them, an old man himself, surrounded by the familiarity of a place to call home. The thought both enlivened and soothed him, and he smiled then to himself as he continued to walk.

In a small town where new arrivals were rare, the sudden appearance of two improbable characters caused quite a stir. So in a way, it was no surprise when the poor boy with his wolf dog wound up in the employ of the equally perplexing carpenter with his mule and his enormous trees.

Joseph had been sitting under a spruce when a commotion in the street drew him from his daydream. Having arrived only four days prior, the boy had not yet witnessed one of Abram's grand entrances – which were made grand only by the reaction of the people, much to Abram's wry amusement – and Joseph was immediately interested in the source of all the commotion. His dog, too, had been roused and sat at attention peering intently into the crowd.

In his unassuming way, Abram was hauling in timber, the log chained to a harness which was draped heavily across his mule's shoulders. The tree in tow rumbled the ground so vigorously as it was dragged along that the people watching could feel it in their feet.

When the mule approached with blinders on, the dog had gone mad. The wildness it had inherited among the sands of the desert had overcome the dog's domestication, and it broke from Joseph's side and lunged at the heels of the harnessed animal.

In an act of defense, the mule kicked violently at its pursuer, but missed, clipping the chain instead. From the impact and load, one chain broke, and the log fell to the dust of the street while the draft animal attempted to break away. One chain had remained intact however, and the mule was restrained. This only made matters worse since the animal was now half-tethered to the log and rearing and bucking violently in an attempt to flee.

The crowd gasped, women screamed and pulled their children away, while the men tried to figure out what to do next. Joseph sprang to action at once, seizing his dog by the scruff of its neck and throwing it to the ground out of the way. The dog, surprised by the authority with which Joseph had acted, did not get back up, and Joseph and Abram were able to quiet the unsettled mule.

As the chaos subsided, the mule settled, and the dog lay in the dirt. Abram and Joseph exchanged names. The boy was horrified at the damage and excitement his dog had caused, and expected to be met with anger and frustration from the older man. But Abram just chuckled, commenting on the unpredictable nature of animals and life, and they at once found a kinship.

Joseph offered to help haul the log the rest of the way to its destination, having no preconception of the work in which Abram was engaged. Abram, exhausted from his journey, accepted.

Together, the two worked to haul the broken end of chain and log to the chapel, and each fell to the dust exhausted upon arrival, even though it was only a few blocks from where the incident had occurred.

Once the log had been unhitched, and the mule watered and put up for the night, the men sat on the steps enjoying a pot of coffee, courtesy of Sister Matilde. They talked of their origins, the hardships they'd endured, the depths they'd known.

Joseph, fresh from the desert, related his life-altering experiences in such vivid detail that a few times, Abram closed his eyes, envisioning the scenes told of by the boy. It was as though they had been friends for years, even though they'd met only an hour before.

The next morning, the sisters found the two men working side by side.

Their first task - the one which Abram had already begun - was to haul in the lumber. He had known from the outset of the project that the native lumber would not suffice for the design he envisioned.

Fortunately, as a wanderer of the lands surrounding the town, he knew where to source the wood he required. And though it grew some hundred and twenty miles from the location of the chapel, there was a sense of purpose that drove him onward in spite of the challenge.

So when he awoke the morning of the first day, he knew that before him lay months of hard work, but of the hard work of carrying out God's will. It was the same curious faith that led Abram - and Sister Matilde - to wonder if God hadn't also sent Joseph to be of assistance.

As the two worked, first to haul in the lumber, and then to begin splitting it, a deep bond began to develop. Joseph was in perpetual awe at the skill and patience of the older man, and Abram in turn admired his pupil's depth of perception, and the way he watched attentively each action in order to mirror it himself.

Joseph learned quickly, which was good, because Abram worked quickly as well. In fact, the speed and agility with which he worked was the reason Abram had never held an apprentice for more than a few days, in spite of his excellent reputation for masterful work.

From his teacher, Joseph learned to split, plane and hone boards. He learned to work with the wood rather than against it, exploiting its weakness while leveraging its strength. He learned to observe the grain and follow the form which had grown into the wood through years of wind and rain. And he learned to see within the raw stock the depth of possibility.

Abram had been a sculptor, but began a trade in woodworking as a way to earn a living when his most reliable patrons set off to live in California, drawn by the gold and the sea. In his new trade, he applied the same sentiment and skills he had developed through sculpting. His work was met immediately with great success.

Joseph developed a similar admiration for the man's art. He also thought it uniquely fortunate that he'd found such fulfilling work, both in the last town and now in this one. Still, the desert had worked its settling magic in his soul, and the feelings of unrest had not returned, even after two months of working day in and day out with Abram.

Strange how I grew to feel so restless where I was the last time, he thought one afternoon while planing a stair tread. And here, it all feels like I could do this forever without getting tired of it. And he wondered if the desert really had changed him for good.

The two slept in simple, single beds in the room in the chapel. Because they were mostly ever working, eating or sleeping, Joseph found few distractions, least of all women. He found a clarity and sureness in directing his full effort and energy towards his purpose, which since coming to the town, had consisted of helping Abram - and the sisters - realize their dream.

After a few hard months, the wood had all been hauled in, split, dried and planed. The dry climate made quick work of the drying, and left hardly any time for rest. By the time a log had been split and set to cure, the boards from the previous log were ready to build into the design.

Joseph learned how to interpret the carpenter's plans, and how to see the whole project in his mind, even when very little existed in the material world.

Often the sisters would come into the chapel to find both craftsmen staring silently at the place the staircase would eventually be placed. Neither spoke, neither moved, but as they went back to their work out front of the colonnade, they each held a renewed vision which gradually began to emerge from the lumber.

Occasionally, while working, with wood shavings in their hair, thick callouses on their hands, and suntanned skin stretched in concentration, they would each look up from their labor. When their eyes caught, a smile would spread across their lips without interrupting their work. As they sawed, planed, sanded, honed, or hewed, their motions rocked with the sway of the breeze blowing in from the desert, still smelling of juniper and sunbake. And in all this it seemed to each of them that they became the embodiment of the timeless eternity, crafting matter out of material the same way the world was created in the first place.

Sister Matilde, though both devout and often very busy, would frequently find excuses to walk past the men while they worked. Though she never said as much, she held a certain fondness for the older carpenter. But it was only fondness, since she considered herself partnered with God.

Perhaps Abram truly didn't notice because he was so singular in his focus on his craft, or perhaps he pretended not to notice because he didn't want to break the spell, but he never acknowledged the uncommon frequency of Sister Matilde's visits. At least not until Joseph asked him chidingly over dinner one evening what he thought of the woman.

Abram stared straight-faced into his mug, still chewing a bite of bread, with the afternoon light slanting through the single stained-glass window of their priestly quarters. A long silence followed in which the man's eyes seemed to glass over. It was as though he went very far away.

Eventually, Abram looked into the boy's eyes and told him, "I am here to help, and love only ever complicates what should be simple. Besides, she's chaste – it's a requirement of the job."

In his voice and in his eyes, Joseph had detected a labored acceptance of a fact more stated than believed. Still, he understood it was not something Abram wished to discuss, and it certainly wouldn't be the sort of thing he would enjoy being teased about, and so the two never spoke of it again.

It was the suffocating heat of August, and the staircase was nearing completion. Each day marked significant progress.

At first, the work had progressed at a pace Joseph found to be excruciatingly slow. Each step seemed to last for days or even weeks, and by the end of each afternoon, all that could be shown for the labor was a growing pile of sawdust and another pile of unfinished pieces. But as they grew nearer and nearer the final construction, their progress seemed to accelerate.

Joseph, with his younger eyes and junior expertise, was set to the final trimming of the steps, the winding stringers, and the pegs which would be used to hold the whole thing together. Abram was exacting in his expectations, and he frequently tossed away components that had taken days to create, just because Joseph had over-trimmed their edges or removed too much material in such a way that the final assembly would be compromised.

The first few times this happened, Joseph felt that familiar feeling of failure, and it settled in the pit of his stomach as he watched his mentor discard his work without the least bit of emotion.

That was how Abram taught: Without stormy emotion, but likewise without compromise. When he noticed a mistake had been made by his apprentice, he would simply take the piece, point out the error, and throw it to the side with the other discards. And so, over time, Joseph became so learned in the ways of the wood and the craft that his mistakes became more and more scarce.

By the time the August sun beat down upon the weathered carpenters, Joseph's craftsmanship had developed so thoroughly that Abram scarcely even inspected the boy's work. Through the old carpenter's teaching, Joseph learned how to see the material, the vision, and was able to discern when a piece had been completed adequately.

The first time Joseph himself discarded a piece because it had failed to meet his own standards, Abram smiled almost inwardly. Joseph had not smiled, however. Instead, with a look of absolute determination, he walked across the portico to the pile of prepared boards and grabbed another, setting to work correcting his mistake.

On August 14th, it came time to raise the stringers and fasten them to the floor and the loft. Abram and Joseph had crafted great curvatures from the heavy timbers, with numerous pieces pegged and jointed, and it took many men to erect the bones. By the end of the day a gaunt skeleton stood in the chapel.

Sister Matilde had come to watch the festivities and remained there in the great hall for a long while after the men had all gone home for supper. That was where Abram found her, sitting on a pew, gazing upon the dream of a staircase with admiration and gratitude.

He sat beside her as she turned to look at him. In her eyes he saw an unrelenting love and longing. He held her gaze for a moment before returning to the staircase.

"Did you hear our prayers?" she asked him, still looking at him, even though he looked only upon his masterwork. Outside was a growing twilight and it made the interior of the chapel very dark. The lights of the candles in their sconces along the wall reflected on his skin and it made him look younger.

"Prayers are only heard by God," he said in response.

She stared a moment longer before also turning her gaze to the stairway and choir loft. It was a strange and beautiful thing to gaze upon a material solution that seemed so unlikely to occur that many had said it couldn't be done. And yet there it was. There stood the staircase that would complete the chapel, and beside her sat the man who had appeared out of nowhere to make it happen.

After a time, Abram turned to her once and smiled, then stood and walked to the front doors. Then he slipped outside without looking back.

Sister Matilde remained in the chapel until late in the evening. There was something transfixing about the apparition of what was to be, and no matter how hard she tried, she couldn't seem to pull herself away.

Abram was troubled. He held within him the same empty sorrow many artists know when their greatest works are nearing completion.

At the rate they were working, the two men would be finished with the project in its entirety before the first chill hung on the morning sun of autumn. And then what would he do? Abram figured it would then be time for him to return from whence he came, and he felt a pensive anguish at leaving behind the adobe town and good company he'd come to know. But he wouldn't stay. That was not for him to decide, anyway.

In addition to the grief over the closing of his best-lived chapter, Abram bore the burden of knowing all these things on Joseph's behalf, even though the boy himself did not know them. He knew from their never-ending conversation that Joseph had never worked so hard, nor with so much dedication, as he had on this.

And he knew that only once one has accomplished something of profound and lasting value are they capable of knowing the emptiness that can exist. It is the emptiness that comes once his dream has left his heart to live amongst the material world, made manifest by effort and good grace.

As he walked through the almost-hot evening, crickets singing in chorus all around him, an uncommon humidity hung on the air. Abram found himself rounding the corner into the stables where his mule had been put up. Walking to the stall door, the animal met him, its great head reaching forth for the alfalfa he held out.

He rubbed the mule's cheek and pressed his forehead to the beast's. There they stayed for a long moment, the scent of hay and cedar thick in the air. A small lantern hung on the post near the stall and Abram lit it with a match from a drawer in the stable desk.

As he stared down the row of stalls towards and out of the open door at the end of the building, some of the weight of his pondering lifted, and he felt a new peace wash over him. He had come for a purpose, and in all the necessary ways the purpose had been fulfilled. The work was not finished, but the purpose had been satisfied, and the boy was more than capable of finishing the job. In fact, the thought occurred to Abram that perhaps it was Joseph's destiny to finish the project alone. The boy had bloomed into an adept craftsman – a master in his own right – and had indeed transformed into a man before the old carpenter's eyes.

No longer was he the boy who wandered on the wind, taking criticism well, but never fostering his own accountability. Now he was the sort of man who lived by his own laws and standards to the betterment of his work and his world. These thoughts brought a smile to Abram's face.

He drew the mule's halter and lead from the nail on the post next to the lantern, placed them over the animal's head and unlatched the stall door. Lantern held out before him, a blanket from a shelf in the stable over his shoulders and the mule's lead rope in his other hand, Abram set out into the night.

It wasn't the first time Abram had gone missing.

When Joseph awoke the next morning to find the other bed empty, he hadn't given much thought as to what might have happened to his mentor and friend. Sometimes he would vanish for several hours or several days, probably off wandering in the desert or searching for some elusive treasure. But he'd always reappear and resume his work just as though he'd never left.

Joseph knew well the work needed to bring the staircase to completion. So after washing his face and hands and eating a crust of bread from the previous night's supper, he straightened his clothes as though he were going to church, combed his hair, and took up the old carpenter's tools.

He worked all morning, placing piece after numbered piece into its place, pegging and gluing as he went, drawing a profound satisfaction from the act of creation. There was not an ounce of hurriedness in his toil, no modicum of haste. Instead, it was with a laborious concentration that he laid each board, set each joint, and pegged each tread.

Every time he watched his hands lay a component in its place he saw within that component all the hours of work that had gone into creating it. He saw the sun and the rain and the sweaty toil of felling and hauling the log to the chapel. He felt the sawdust beneath his fingernails and smelled the fine shavings from the spokeshave as they fell softly upon the dusty ground like downy feathers from a torn pillow.

He saw too the dedication with which Abram had taught him, and the patience he had learned as a result. He saw in each successful curve the ten failed attempts it had taken to arrive at such elegance.

By the end of the day when Sister Matilde called Joseph to supper, Abram had not returned. Joseph thought to ask the sister if she knew anything of his whereabouts, but recalled the seemingly sensitive nature of their relationship and decided not to. Instead, he took his meal of soup and bread and ate in silence on the front steps of the chapel, the evening sun still sweltering as it filtered through tired cedar trees in the chapel's courtyard.

With such intentionality and meticulous care permeating his day, he felt serene sitting there consuming the good food. It was as though his entire existence in that moment had become a meditation – a prayer – a celebration of the possibilities of life itself. He breathed in through his nose and caught the scent of sage and juniper on the wind.

For the first time in months, he saw again the face of the woman from his dream in the desert. It was a flash, hardly intelligible. But he saw and felt at once that she was near. He even thought he caught the hint of her scent on the breeze. It was the same scent he'd smelled that night as he stumbled from the bar, unknowingly walking towards his assailant, and toward the rest of his life.

It was inexplicable how settled he became in his chest. It was the belief that this woman existed somewhere in the world, and that they were each on a blind, divinely orchestrated collision course. His belief fortified him, and he drew a deep breath of the warm, late evening sunshine as a breeze picked up and whistled its caress through his hair.

It had been nearly a week and still Abram had not reappeared. With each day the sun rose, Joseph had continued to work dutifully, though he also felt a growing acceptance in his soul that perhaps the old carpenter would never return.

With the acknowledgement of this possibility, there grew a sadness, not at the loss of his friend, and certainly not because of fear for his wellbeing, but because he found it tragic the way so many craftsmen disappeared from the earth mere moments before the completion of their greatest works.

He recalled the way Sister Anna's grandfather had died during the final expressions of his clock. He saw it so much like the way Abram had mysteriously disappeared just before his staircase vision would be realized. And he began to think of his own life, as well. How he'd abandoned his own death moments before it claimed him, choosing instead to live. How he had left Mary behind in that lovely town, in spite of the love he'd felt for her.

He thought about how he had abandoned his craft in the clockmaker's shop, leaving Sister Anna alone with her legacy entrusted only to the young, loyal Gabriel.

Perhaps we cannot live with our own success any more than we can live with our failures, he thought. Perhaps when we approach anything that threatens to redefine our existence, we choose to retreat. He chose in that moment to stick things out and see.

Joseph had been eating alone on the front steps again. As he walked back through the chapel to return the plate and cup to Sister Matilde, he paused to gaze upon the staircase. It was there that she met him, striding in as smoothly as a ghost. There they stood – Sister Matilde and Joseph – side by side, admiring the masterwork together.

"I don't think we're going to see him again," Joseph said, but it was passing between both of their hearts simultaneously.

The sister exhaled slowly.

Joseph turned to her, and placing his hand upon her shoulder, looked into her eyes. He noticed for the first time how beautiful they were, how full of life. The candlelight reflecting off them, the scent of sawdust and faint incense in the air, he felt a tremendous appreciation for the woman, and in his state of vulnerability, he sensed her heartbreak.

After a moment in stillness, he spoke softly but certainly, saying, "I will finish this work, and then I will stay to care for this place. It is what Abram would have wanted, and what I have been put in this town – on this earth – to do. I've spent a lot of time running from life, as people often do, and I saw tonight that my time of running is done."

She smiled, and he couldn't tell exactly what heaviness lay within her heart. A mixture of anguish, despair and reverence hung on her lips. After a time, she simply nodded and smiled earnestly, thanked the boy, and took from him his dishes.

It was a Saturday in October when Joseph lay the final tread at the top of the staircase. With very little ado at all, he tapped the edge with his mallet and smiled as it settled into place. He took one deep breath and let it fall as he looked over the empty room below. The autumn light streamed through the stained-glass windows on the east side. All was still.

No more sounds of saws or hammers, no more settling dust, no more mule's chains. The dog lay in a slant of sunlight against the wall outside the open door, and, suddenly aware of the new silence, it raised its head to look towards the boy.

In the depths of completion, Joseph felt at once a fullness and a vast emptiness. For a moment he felt a panic rise within him. Without his work before him he felt as though the world would continue to spin, and he would remain forever anchored there at the top of the stairs in some chapel in a southwest town half covered in dust.

His legacy had been secured, but there was nothing left to do. He took another deep breath and settled his restlessness. He remembered his promise to remain and care for the chapel. To live as the humble servant to the sisters. To settle into commitment and to learn how not to run. One ending is always another beginning, he thought.

He descended the stairs in a sort of trance, his fingers following the grain and joints he knew so well. It was as though he explored his own body in experiencing the completed work. Each inch he knew, and yet in its wholeness it was transformed, foreign and new.

He was standing in the crisp light of the autumn midmorning when Sister Matilde entered from the door behind the pulpit, speaking softly.

"And right in here is the most beautiful miracle of my entire life. It is not quite finished, so you may have to use your imagination, but I assure you it won't be difficult."

"Actually, Sister," Joseph interjected without turning around, "it is finished."

As he turned slowly to see the expression on her face, he was blindsided by a completely different sight.

Walking arm in arm with Sister Matilde was a woman. When he gazed upon her, the light through the stained-glass became blinding and brilliant. The room took on colors never seen by human eyes, and the walls in which the windows were hung began to resonate with the sounds of angels.

Joseph saw in a vivid, furious picture show of memory and foretelling the woman before him woven throughout his life. He felt her face in his hands, her head upon his shoulder, her presence next to him through the tumultuous chaos of life. He saw in her eyes the fire he'd

216

found within himself, and it spoke to him, drawing him in.

Sister Matilde was introducing the two, explaining how the young woman would be the new choir director, and how fitting it was that the loft's staircase had been finished on the very day she had come.

But Joseph heard none of this, because his eyes and everything else about him was transfixed by the woman before him. She, too, seemed unable to look away from him. And then she extended her hand and smiled, and he took it in his for the first time.

The End

Acknowledgements

True gratitude cannot be contained in words. Pages groan under the enormous burden of earnest thanks. Still, there are those whose contributions to this story are too great not to receive mention here.

For their encouragement, faith, and unyielding support, I thank my mother, father, and brother, Donna, David, and Jonah Greene. And for her relentless patience in the face of my literary obsession, her tolerance of my 4:30am writing ritual, and her superb company, I thank Danielle DeSalvo.

For her selfless, generous work in helping me with the first versions of this manuscript, for her hours of reading and editing and constructive correspondence, and especially for her kind words of uplifting belief in my potential, I thank Gwen Diehn.

And to all those who have nurtured my unseasonable confidence and voracious writing habit over the years, thank you.

A Note from the Author

First of all, thank *you* for reading. Embarking upon a journey with someone new is an act of courage and faith in itself, and I'm humbled you've chosen to do so with me, and with the characters that have come from my heart. The story of how this book came to be is, in itself, a special one to me. I'll start at the beginning.

Writing was never something I thought of as more than an occasional hobby – a playful endeavor to be pulled out a few times each year when I was feeling particularly expressive. Usually this took place in journals, but once in a while, I published my pieces in quiet little corners of the internet, on personal blogs. Sometimes I'd read a book. Mostly I ignored literature altogether.

In 2019, I was a year-and-a-half into single fatherhood, my marriage of five years having ended the January before. As I pieced together the remnants of who I wanted to be outside of my marriage, I began to realize I could not identify any deeper purpose for my life. Mine was a directionless future, and I didn't like it at all.

So, inspired by the vision quests of Indigenous peoples across the globe and lured by the quiet gravity of the wild I went into the desert alone for four days. I didn't eat. I drank little water. I slept under the stars, I wandered the sand and stone. I made my way from just north of Moab, Utah, to a little ways south of it.

During that time I found myself slowly losing grip on reality as I knew it. Dreams and visions and waking seemed to flow seamlessly with each other. I was along for the ride.

I, like Joseph, traveled with a dog. Once or twice, that dog ran off into the desert and I didn't see him for hours at a time. One night, I slept in a cave before a fire, and he didn't return until the middle of the night. The dog's name was Badger. He will doubtless make his way into other stories of mine in the future.

Many of Joseph's dreams and visions are very similar to those I experienced myself, adapted to fit his story a little better. The dream he has on his last night in the desert – the dream of the woman – is an adaptation of a short story I wrote following my own dream of a woman in the desert. That story can be found in the pages following this note.

When I emerged, having finally eaten for the first time in over 96 hours, I knew frustratingly little about my purpose. As I drove across the mountains to Colorado, I was frustrated, feeling that I'd learned nothing, because it felt at the time that I was no closer to understanding my life's purpose.

All I knew, or believed I knew, was that I'd meet a woman. If dreams are to be believed, I felt she'd be important to my journey, and that her name was Mackenzie. These were the details I'd gained from vision of the woman.

In February, following my desert experience, I was synchronistically introduced to Mackenzie. We began dating in March. And though we parted ways in July of the same year, the four months that we were together changed the course of my life forever. Mackenzie saw me as a writer, even when I didn't, and she seemed to draw it out of me. She encouraged me. Coaxed the words from my soul and pushed for me to put them down on paper. She wrote, too. Beautifully. We'd cook dinner and write together. It was our rhythm.

While I was with her, I wrote and published prolifically, and I started writing a book. This book, about a lost boy who finds himself in the desert of the American west. So now, I keep writing, and I have come to feel as though perhaps it is my purpose to spend my time on earth spinning stories that help others make sense of their own confusion, their own aimlessness, their own frustrating stuck-ness.

The road to destiny is winding, full of blind corners and harrowing hairpin turns. But we walk on anyway, because if we don't, we find ourselves rather stuck-feeling. Here's hoping your own journey is filled with excitement, struggle, triumph, and deepest satisfaction.

Thank you again for reading.

The Original Short Story
that Inspired the Novel

He awoke suddenly, alert and awake, listening intently to the silence of the desert canyon sleeping around him. No beasts padded through camp, no wind swayed the branches of the pinion pine, carrying the scent of juniper to his nose. No chorus of coyotes howled at the moonless sky. Even the stars were resting, their normal tinkling of bells hushed against the chill of the late autumn air.

He lay staring up at the sky for a while, considering intently the dream which had roused his body and heart wide awake.

Sitting up, he was struck by the vivid clarity with which the features of the canyon walls presented themselves to him, even on a night as dark as this. The chill came ferociously, gnawing at his bones but he fended it off calmly.

He looked around himself, gazing upon the navy blanket of sky, full of holes, resting so perfectly atop the cliffs and caves of his canyon. The desert absorbs light and stores it for later, the same way it does with water, he thought to himself. Or perhaps it was not so much a thought as a knowing welling up within him, a gift from some mystic force beyond his understanding.

Closing his eyes as his chest heaved a greedy gulp of crisp, dry oxygen, her face flashed before his mind's eye behind his eyelids. He lingered there, gazing into her eyes, fierce with fury and glowing with the uninhibited spark of youthful optimism. She was beautiful. Her slender nose reminding him of a beautiful wildness he felt within his own soul, her brow and cheekbones telling stories of her strength. He had never seen this face before tonight, in his dream, and yet she was somehow familiar. He had dreamed her, and yet he knew her.

The boy had heard tales of past lives, and had wondered at their accuracy. Sorcerers and alchemists had made frequent mention in books he'd read of the energetic ties we carry from one life to the next, or of a person's ability to know about things beyond the scope of his personal, lived experience. He'd had no reason to doubt them, but with this mysterious woman's face flitting before his, he had discovered a reason to believe.

Re-opening his eyes he allowed the softness of his sight to rest upon the majesty of the canyon. He had met Her, and he knew she was out there, somewhere, awaiting his invitation. "You'll know her when you see her, and she you," said a voice inside his heart. It was the playful, knowing sort of voice that comes from a heart delighted by the unpredictable nature of love.

The night, still deep in transit between dusk and dawn, seemed at odds with his level of alertness. Many times his body had awoken just before dawn, feeling the jubilation of the coming day, but this was not that sort of situation, and it perplexed him slightly. Returning to his blankets in order to sleep until daybreak seemed a waste of a beautiful moment, and so he decided to gather the little wood remaining from the night before and build a small fire.

Laying the frayed bark of an ancient juniper across the glowing embers of his dinner fire, a meager flame arose quickly and without much ado. He stoked it with the wing of an owl – a gift to him from an old shaman – and laid down a few split pine logs to lend their strength to the growing flame.

The glow, the crackle and the warmth soothed him away from the alertness which had irritated his soul upon waking. In the distance he heard the hoot of an owl and the scamper of a hare, betrayed by its fear and running for its life. Little noises seemed much larger in that canyon. Even his breath could be heard echoing off the cliffs, or perhaps the rock was just breathing with him. On a night such as this, one can never be sure, he thought.

As he watched the flame, fixating on its dance, wild and free, unbound by any expectations or woes, he thought of love. He pondered his past lovers and wondered how they were getting on. He thought, as the edges of his lips rose upwards in a reminiscing smile, of the good memories and less-happy memories as well. All ends as it is meant to end. Even the dark nights eventually relent, giving way to the light, he thought.

As he meandered through the memories stored within his own heart, he returned eventually to the face of the woman from his dream. She was calling to him from afar, urging him into action, pleading with smiling eyes for him to rise to his full potential, shine his brightest light, and sing loudly his most beautiful song, so that she might be drawn to him as the needle of a compass is drawn dutifully to its guiding star. He understood. The path had been set many years ago. He was being offered, on this most spectacular of nights, the opportunity to gaze into the crystal ball of that ethereal mystic and see a glimpse of what his life would hold.

He sat near the fire with his eyes closed for a long time. Perhaps he fell asleep. After a time of dozing, a crimson sun roused him. Visions are wonderful things, thought the boy as he opened his eyes to see the first light of dawn rising over the eastern wall. But one day, it will be this night that exists only in my heart, and she will be there resting on my shoulder as I open my eyes, as real as the sand on which I sit and the sun which rises over that ridge.

He knew where he was going, or rather to whom, and so he packed camp, and set off in search of this mysterious woman who had transformed him in one, simple, solitary night.